THE ROGUE

by

Jonas Saul

PUBLISHED BY:
Imagine Press Inc.
Ebook ISBN: 978-1-927404-30-0
Paperback ISBN: 978-1-998047-29-1
Hardcover ISBN: 978-1-998047-30-7

The Sarah Roberts Series

Dark Visions (One)
The Warning (Two)
The Crypt (Three)
The Hostage (Four)
The Victim (Five)
The Enigma (Six)
The Vigilante (Seven)
The Rogue (Eight)
Killing Sarah (Nine)
The Antagonist (Ten)
The Redeemed (Eleven)
The Haunted (Twelve)
The Unlucky (Thirteen)
The Abandoned (Fourteen)
The Cartel (Fifteen)
Losing Sarah (Sixteen)
The Pact (Seventeen)
The Terror (Eighteen)
The Chase (Nineteen)
The Betrayal (Twenty)
Sarah's Return (Twenty-One)
The Hunt (Twenty-Two)
The Delivery (Twenty-Three)
The Trap (Twenty-Four)
The Ultimatum (Twenty-Five)
The Depraved (Twenty-Six)
The Condemned (Twenty-Seven)
Payback (Twenty-Eight)
The Unknown (Twenty-Nine)
Wrath (Thirty)
The Damned (Thirty-One)
The Game (Thirty-Two)

The Decoy (Thirty-Three)
The Disappearance (Thirty-Four)
The Whole Truth (Thirty-Five)
Alex (Thirty-Six)
Parkman (Thirty-Seven)
Darwin (Thirty-Eight)
Aaron (Thirty-Nine)
Remains To Be Seen (Forty)

The Jake Wood Novels

The Immortal Gene (Book One)
The Immortal Target (Book Two)

Standalone Novels

'Til Death Do Us Part
The Drowning
The Woman in the Woods
The Threat
The Specter
The Mafia Trilogy
A Murder in Time
Frequency of the Dead

Co-Authored Novels

Collision Course (Written with Gary Ponzo)
There Will Be Blood (Written with Rania Stone)
The Soulless (Written with Rania Stone)

Short Story Collections

Twisted Fate (Tales of Horror)

The Rogue

Twists of Fate (Tales of Hope)

Chapter 1

PARKMAN REFUSED TO BELIEVE that Sarah Roberts was dead. He would have to see the body with his own eyes. There could be no other way. Vivian, her dead sister, would've protected Sarah. It was Vivian who sent her on sojourns that came with a degree of danger, but Sarah always walked away. Injuries, yes. Broken bones, sure. But death? Never.

How could Sarah be killed doing Vivian's bidding? It wasn't right.

Parkman fiddled with a toothpick that hung loosely from his mouth. He leaned back in the airplane seat and waited for the plane to taxi into the Fiumicino Airport gate in Rome. A rental car waited for him.

A few days ago, while investigating details for Sarah, he had discovered new information but couldn't get a hold of her. After waiting patiently to hear from her and monitoring the Italian news of the area she was in, he had read about an explosion in a restaurant that had leveled it and the hotel above it in the historical center of Umbertide, Italy.

The names of the deceased weren't listed in the news article, but Parkman knew Sarah had to be connected in some way. After four hours of calls to the Italian authorities in Umbertide, he finally got through to an American stationed there, working a case. A man named Scott McPherson. Scott told Parkman that one of the deceased was, in fact, an American girl named Sarah Roberts and preferred if he could stop calling every officer in Italy about it. Since Parkman knew Sarah and was a former police officer, McPherson asked if he could come to Italy to positively identify the body so next of kin could be notified.

Parkman bought the next ticket out of the San Francisco Airport. That was twelve hours ago, and one layover in Amsterdam.

A wobbly tear escaped his eye, drifted down his cheek, and dropped to his wrist.

Oh, Sarah, I'm so sorry I wasn't there for you. I'm so sorry ...

Chapter 2

Fɪᴠᴇ ᴅᴀʏs ʙᴇғᴏʀᴇ …

"Come this way," Sarah Roberts whispered loud enough for Aaron to hear.

They jumped from the balcony of his second-floor apartment. Sarah ducked under it for cover. Aaron followed and nudged up close.

Above them, men clambered onto Aaron's balcony and spoke in hushed tones. Any second, they would jump off the balcony in pursuit.

She bumped his arm again and whispered, "This way."

She worked her way along the building, staying close to the brick wall. The cold didn't bother her. Running didn't bother her. Her gun, still in the apartment, bothered her. It should be on her. She might as well be naked.

Aaron stayed right at her heels as they turned the corner

of the building. She moved in the shadows, leading him toward the front of the building where they might find cover under a vehicle or behind a large tree until the car FBI Agent Penn Kierian had sent could pick them up.

Before dropping off the balcony, just as their apartment door burst open, she counted seven well-trained, well-armed men in assault gear.

How could the one man in Italy she had agreed to hunt down as a consultant with the FBI locate Aaron's apartment in Toronto and organize an attack within days? How powerful and connected could Sam "The Dealer" Marconi be?

He had to be quite connected to pull this off. Once she was in his sights, he would never go away until she ended it, until she executed him. Tonight's threat only made her want to increase the pressure on him. She wanted to kill The Dealer with her own hands for coming after Aaron.

"Slow down," she whispered. "I have to ensure they don't have men waiting for us at the front."

An organized attack would have the building surrounded. But so far, she hadn't detected anyone on the ground.

At the corner, she had Aaron watch their back as she peeked around it. A four-door Lincoln sat parked at the front of the building. A young couple was getting out, thanking whoever was still inside for the lovely evening.

Nothing else moved.

If men were watching the front, they were well hidden.

The Lincoln pulled away, stopped at the exit, and turned onto the road, moving slowly in the light snow that fell around them.

She turned back to Aaron. "I can't be sure, but it looks

clear upfront. Our ride isn't here yet."

"We need a place to hide. Those guys are going to be here at any moment—"

Scuffling sounded behind them.

They looked at each other.

"Shit," Sarah said. "Let's move. Go!"

Sarah led the way around to the front of the apartment building just as The Dealer's advance team rounded the corner thirty feet behind them.

All the way up the sidewalk, she thanked the skies that the snow hadn't fallen fast enough to make the sidewalk slippery yet.

A horn blared on the street.

A car spun out as it tried to enter the access road to the building. Its tires spun in search of purchase, the car slid sideways until a snow bank arrested its slide. The engine revved, and the vehicle propelled forward.

The driver was in the kind of hurry one of Kierian's men would be in. Sarah headed toward the car, knowing it was their only chance.

Aaron turned toward the car at the same time.

Someone shouted behind them, but Sarah couldn't make out what was said over the wind. Heavy breathing added pressure to her damaged ribs. She winced with each inhalation. When the pain slowed her down, Aaron grabbed her arm and helped her toward the Impala headed their way.

"Stop, or I'll shoot," a man yelled.

A weapon fired behind them.

"Damn it," she shouted and ducked instinctively. If the rescue car were any farther away, she would've dove into the snow bank on the side of the access road, but it was too close to stop now. "Keep low and zigzag."

"I'm not letting you go," Aaron shouted back.

She yanked her arm out of his grasp and pulled away. "Make less of a target of yourself or get shot." She spun left, then right, her head down. "Your choice."

Another weapon fired behind them. She glanced at Aaron to see if he got hit, but he was still running.

The Impala stopped. The back door on the passenger side popped open. The driver righted himself and rolled the front window down.

"Hurry," the driver shouted.

The front lobby of the apartment building filled with men in black body armor and assault rifles.

What the hell? Sarah dove into the back seat of the car, her ribs screaming in protest.

Aaron landed hard behind her, and the driver hit the gas, spinning toward the exit, almost losing control on the way out of the parking lot.

Automatic weapons fire filled the night. Sarah kept her head down, her eyes squeezed shut. Aaron leaned into her, the upper half of his body on the carpeted floor of the car, his legs upside down in the seat.

The car hit a bump, swerved to right itself, and shot forward.

Sarah opened her eyes and winced at the fresh pain in her ribs. She and Aaron sat up.

Sarah watched behind them, the back window still intact, the figures in black retreating.

"Just in time, eh?" the driver said over the wind coming in through the open passenger window.

Sarah slapped Aaron on the arm. "Next time, give me

Vivian's note right away." She breathed in shallow breaths to keep from expanding her ribs too much. "We almost got killed back there."

He leaned away from her, his face a mask of regret. "I'm sorry. I totally thought it was about something in the future. You know, something that could wait."

"It was about something in our future, wingnut. Something in our near future."

"I know that now." He looked out the back window. "What's a wing nut?"

"You. Right now, you're a wingnut. Your fuck up could've gotten us killed."

"You two almost done back there?"

"Who are you?" Sarah asked.

"Your driver."

"No. Give me a name."

He met her eyes in the mirror but didn't say anything.

"Who sent you?" she asked.

"Kierian."

"I need your cell phone, so I can call him and ream his ass out. No one was supposed to know about the Italian trip."

The driver slowed and turned onto a quiet side street a few blocks up from the apartment building.

It dawned on Sarah that she hadn't heard any police sirens. With all that gunfire, how come no one in the apartment building called the police? And with hired killers, how come none of them hit the car even once with that much shooting?

Something didn't add up.

Her suspicion of the driver increased.

"Do you have a name?" she asked. "A cell phone?"

"Of course," he said. "Just give me a sec." He looked at the empty seat beside him. "It's here somewhere."

Sarah and Aaron exchanged a glance.

The driver stopped the car. "Here it is." He turned around and brought his hand up to the top of the seat.

A silver-plated Magnum faced them from two feet away.

"I found my cell phone." He looked at his gun. "Although the only call you can make with this is the call to heaven. Or hell, whichever you're destined to go to."

Sarah leaned back in the seat a few inches but knew it didn't matter. Aaron's hands twitched in his lap. If he was going to attempt to disarm the guy, she only hoped he was successful. It would be hard for the driver to miss either one of them from this distance.

"Are you two ever stupid," the driver said. "That was the easiest grab we've ever done. You ran right into my car."

"Did Kierian set this up?" Sarah asked.

The driver laughed without taking his eyes off her. "The stupid meter just keeps going higher."

"Call her stupid again, and I'll shove that gun up your ass," Aaron whispered.

The driver's face turned serious. He angled the gun toward Aaron and moved it closer.

"We came for her, not you. One more wise crack out of your face, and I'll remove it for you."

"Where are the sirens?" Sarah asked to get his attention back on her. "Is that why no shots hit the car? Because you're in on it with them?"

"Maybe you're not so stupid after all," he said. Aaron and the driver locked eyes. Without averting his gaze from Aaron, he said, "It was staged."

"Staged?" She needed his attention back on her if Aaron was to make a grab for the gun. "What do you mean, staged?"

He faced her, his gun aimed at Aaron from a foot away.

"Just filming a movie. We've got the permit and everything. All the weapons carried blanks. Not a single live round." He paused and glanced down at his Magnum. "Except this one."

"Are you saying we just jumped off our balcony and ran around the building only to jump into your car while men shot blanks at us?"

"That's exactly what I'm saying."

"Don't worry about Aaron. I'm the one who's going to shove that fucking gun up your ass."

"Watch your mouth, pretty lady, or I'll wash it out with my dick."

"Speaking of dicks, you guys interrupted us," Sarah said. "We were about to have the best sex this side of Jupiter when Kierian called. Oh, wait, that was Kierian, right?"

"We don't know who tipped you off," the driver said. "But that doesn't matter. Enough with the small talk. I've got a message for you."

"A message," Sarah said, rubbing her hands together. "Oh, this oughta be good."

Aaron looked ready to spring, but she knew he would wait until he was absolutely sure the Magnum could be removed as a threat.

"Sam Marconi wants you to know you're not welcome in Italy."

"Well, tell Mr. Marconi that—"

"I'm not finished!" the driver shouted.

Aaron flinched. The driver brought the gun up and pressed it into Aaron's forehead. "Hold on there, partner. Don't be stupid."

"What else is there?" Sarah asked.

"If you come to Italy, you won't survive twenty-four hours. That's what I'm supposed to tell you."

"You're joking, right? Because that's the kind of thing that'll make me want to go even more."

"Oh, man," the driver smirked. "Are you ever stupid." When he said stupid, he pressed the Magnum harder into Aaron's forehead, forcing his head back. "If Marconi can get to you here, how do you think you'll survive on his soil?"

"You don't know me very well, and neither does he. Are we done yet?"

"Just watch what you eat."

"Watch what we eat? What's that supposed to mean?"

"I have no idea, but you're supposed to be told—"

A hand extended into the open passenger window and placed a large handgun against the driver's temple.

"Drop your weapon," the familiar voice said.

Kierian.

"Fuck you. Drop yours, or I'll shoot this kid's brains all over the back window."

Aaron's eyes widened. Sarah ran through her options.

"Fine," Kierian said. "Take it easy. We'll do it your way."

His handgun slowly pulled away from the driver's temple. As it did, the driver eased off enough that Aaron could straighten his head.

When a weapon discharged, Sarah jolted and dropped her head between her knees. Aaron had done the same.

The driver wailed as blood seeped out his wrist. His gun

lay on the floor mats between Aaron's legs. Sarah lunged over and retrieved it.

"It's probably filled with blanks like the rest of their weapons."

The driver held up his arm and screamed as he examined the hole in his wrist.

Sarah aimed the Magnum and fired. The bullet tore through the palm of the driver's hand and busted through the car's windshield.

The driver screamed, his voice cracking.

"Oh, shit," Sarah shouted. "It really was loaded. Sorry about that."

As Kierian opened the side door, Aaron leaned over the seat and drove his fist down hard and fast. The driver went quiet.

Aaron scooted across the seat and hopped out of the car. Sarah followed him, slipping the Magnum into the back of her pants.

"What the hell just happened?" Aaron asked.

Kierian shrugged. "I'm as stunned as you two. Come on. We'll talk in my car."

"Can we trust you?" Aaron asked.

"Of course, you can." He looked at Sarah. "Right?"

"Don't look at me. I trust no one."

Aaron turned to her.

"Except you, of course." She smiled.

"We need to move," Kierian pleaded.

"How did they find us so easily?" Aaron asked. "Who opened their mouth? Who talked?"

"No one talked," Kierian said. "Look, we can discuss this all night if you want, but not here. We have to leave."

Aaron turned to Sarah. "Should we go with this guy? Or would that put us in more danger?"

Sarah reached out her hand. "Kierian, give me your gun."

"You can't be serious."

"Give it to me or see you later. That's the deal."

"Fine." Kierian dropped the weapon in Sarah's open palm.

She handed it to Aaron and showed him where the safety was. "Shoot him if he gives any indication he's not on our side."

"No problem."

"Has it really come to this?" Kierian asked.

"And that's a question you're asking me?"

"Whatever." Kierian started walking. He stopped and turned around. "You two coming?"

"We were about to ten minutes ago, but now the night's fucked."

Sarah tapped Aaron's shoulder, the adrenaline wearing off. "Let's go see what he has to say."

Chapter 3

KIERIAN'S CAR WAS THE same Impala from when Sarah met him the week before.

Aaron, having just had a loaded gun jammed into his forehead in the same color, make, and model of vehicle almost shot Kierian for the cruel joke. When Sarah noticed his hand twitch, she punched his arm and shook her head violently.

"He's a real FBI agent," she said. "Don't even pretend to shoot him."

Aaron grunted but kept the gun down. Once in the back seat of the car, Aaron relinquished Kierian's weapon by dropping it over the passenger seat.

"Thanks," Kierian said and got the car moving. "Let me call this in. I'll be on the phone for a few minutes. We'll talk when we get where we're going."

"Where are we going?" Sarah asked.

"To talk."

"Kierian." She said his name with caution in her voice. "Don't be cryptic, and don't answer my questions that way."

"What way?"

"Stop the car. We're done."

"Okay, okay." He hit his turn signal and headed south on Jarvis toward the Gardiner Expressway. "While I make my calls, I'm driving us north of Toronto to a coffee shop at a Petro-Canada gas station. We'll have privacy there because no one will know where we are. That work for you two?"

She looked out the window in an attempt to hold her tongue. Kierian got on his phone and started talking to someone, asking whoever it was how this evening's events could have possibly taken place.

Aaron's life had just been threatened. Sarah couldn't have that on her conscience. Somehow she had to remove Aaron from the equation, and the only way to do that was to use Kierian's resources to get him into protective custody until Sam "The Dealer" Marconi was neutralized.

She made a few hard decisions about what needed to be done, as Kierian argued with someone on the phone while driving them north on Highway 400.

The large Petro-Canada sign lit up the dark sky as Kierian pulled onto the long exit ramp. He drove around back and parked between two long haulers. The snow had stopped this far north of Toronto, and the parking lot was clear.

Kierian turned to look at them. "Let's get a coffee and something to eat."

They followed Kierian in the side door where a few fast-food shops surrounded a Tim Horton's coffee outlet. Kierian was buying, so they both got large coffees, bagels, and muffins.

At the table, Kierian started.

"Look, I want to tell you both how sorry I am about what happened tonight. But because it did, that advances our timetable and changes things a little."

"How so?" Aaron asked.

Kierian looked at Aaron briefly and then met Sarah's eyes. "Keep an open mind with what I'm about to tell you."

"Of course," Sarah said, smiling wide. "We're all ears."

"Why do you seem so pissed at me?" Kierian asked.

"Pandora's box just opened," Sarah said. She took a large bite of her bagel and washed it down with warm, soothing coffee. "You sure you want a real answer to that question?"

"No, actually, I don't."

"Too late." She swallowed the food in her mouth. "You're going to hear what I have to say because you're the reason we're in this predicament."

"Okay, but I—"

"Shhh," Sarah said, raising a finger to her lips. "Honor the speaker. I've got the floor. We clear?"

He nodded and sipped his coffee. Written all over his face was the embarrassment of being talked to this way.

"You said to me in Detective Lyson's office a few days ago when I agreed to come on board that I wouldn't be left out in the cold and that, in an advisory capacity, I work with the FBI now. Is that correct? Nod or shake your head. Don't test me right now because I'm pretty pissed."

Kierian nodded. He held his coffee cup with both hands but didn't sip it this time.

"Would you agree that Aaron and I were left out in the cold tonight, literally?"

He nodded.

"You said, on that fateful day, that if something were to happen, I would have backup and access to massive resources, *and* I could have a weapon if needed. Correct?"

Kierian turned and watched a group of people coming in from the cool night.

"Is what I said a fair recollection?" Sarah asked.

He sipped his coffee and set the cup down, then nodded.

Aaron remained quiet beside her.

"Finally, this man we're going to Italy to locate has murdered Cosa Nostra men. You told me four other agents had already gone to Italy but came home in body bags. Now, this evening, within days of my agreeing to come on board, Aaron's apartment was attacked in a very organized way, all just to give me a message. Would you say that about sums it up?"

Kierian nodded and opened his mouth to speak. Sarah raised her hand.

Aaron fidgeted beside her. She turned to him. "You'll get your turn." Then back to Kierian. "I understood that I would have the protection of the FBI while in Rome. But yet, even the FBI can't protect itself. I'm sorry—I'm not trying to be rude or speak ill of the dead—I'm simply painting a picture of how serious the man we're going after is."

"I understand," Kierian slipped in.

"Then tell me, who is this guy, and how could he be so connected to know about Aaron Sand me? The kind of power we're talking about is enormous. His resources must be vast. And if you don't have that kind of information in your files, then your files are incomplete, and we're going after someone who we really don't know enough about."

Kierian waited. Aaron looked between the two of them.

"I'm done," Sarah said. "For now."

"Our files are extensive, but you do have a point. It seems he's more resourceful than we previously thought. Also, I stand behind what I said in Lyson's office. The protection offered to you is right here. I showed up. I pulled you out of that car."

"Yeah, but how did it get that far? We were duped and found ourselves in a car driven by one of Marconi's men. When you called to warn us, you said a driver was coming to pick us up. What happened to him?"

"Car accident. He was run off the road six blocks from Aaron's apartment building. After I called to warn you, I got in my car. When I couldn't raise my driver on the phone, I doubled my speed. As I approached, I saw two people get into an Impala that drove out of the building's parking like its ass was on fire. I made an assumption that it was you two getting into the wrong car."

"So it was dumb luck that you got there when you did? That doesn't make me feel any better, and it doesn't inspire a lot of faith in the FBI having our back."

"Evidently, we'll have to make some changes."

"What will Aaron do? They know who he is now. He has a life here, a dojo where he teaches martial arts to hundreds of students. He can't be brought in like this. Nor can he live in protective custody. This has the potential to ruin his life."

She glanced at Aaron, a tear in her eye.

I'm so sorry my life has spilled into yours.

"I understand all that, and we're working on it. I called certain people in the car on the way here. We're attempting to see how Marconi could do this. A full investigation will take place to determine who requested the permit to shoot a movie and stage this entire thing. We'll get to the bottom of it and close the loophole or whatever it is that allowed this to happen."

"And in the meantime? What do we do? What does Aaron do?"

"I don't know. I'm sorry, but I don't." Kierian looked at Aaron. "You're welcome to go back to your life. I'm convinced Sarah was the target. You won't be at risk if Sarah isn't with you or in your apartment."

Aaron had finished his coffee and was fiddling with the lid. "I'll be fine. I can even have one of my other instructors at the dojo stay with me for a few weeks. But what gets me is how serious these guys are."

"What do you mean?" Kierian asked.

"Are you sure Sarah should be involved in hunting criminals of this nature—"

"Are you serious, Aaron?" Sarah's mouth dropped open. "What did we just talk about earlier this evening? You know why I do what I do. So that assholes like the one who orchestrated tonight's festivities are put behind bars."

Aaron turned in his seat and met her eyes. Worry coursed through the lines on his forehead.

Sarah continued, "After what happened tonight, all Marconi did was motivate me even further to bring him down. Nothing will stop me now. How could we ever feel safe with someone that powerful out there running around?"

"You're right, Sarah," Aaron said. "But why you?"

She shook her head and looked down at her half-eaten bagel. "I've been asking myself that same question for years."

"Look, guys, we have to get to Italy as soon as possible. There are people in Rome who can help us. We have an investigative reporter who has information to share, and a high-ranking politician in the Italian Green Party wants to divulge information on Marconi. We need to get there, hear them out, and decide our next move. Agreed?"

"Absolutely," Sarah said. "Sitting around here, on the other side of the ocean, is too risky. It's better to run into the enemy's lair and be done with it."

"Does that mean you agree, or you don't agree?" Kierian asked.

"I'm sarcastic because I'm pissed at what happened tonight. If it were just me, I would be calmer, nicer. But when I saw that weapon jammed into Aaron's forehead … I just felt responsible. I'm pissed off, but I agree. Let's go to Rome. End this thing right now."

"We can fly out in the morning."

"What happens to Aaron in the meantime?" Sarah asked.

"That's up to Aaron."

"What are you saying?" Aaron asked.

"Do you want protective custody until this is over, or maybe an agent could move into your apartment? What would give you peace and comfort?"

"Having Sarah come home with me."

"Not going to happen, Aaron," Sarah said. "You know me better than that."

"Then I want no one in my life. I can take care of myself. They're after you guys, not me. If I feel I'm being watched or something, I'll call the authorities like anyone else would."

"Then it's settled," Kierian said. "We'll get a hotel room by the airport for the night. In the morning, I'll arrange to have tickets at the airport and, Aaron, you can drive my car back home. Deal?"

They nodded in unison. Sarah wondered what Aaron was thinking but was sure he would tell her everything at the hotel later when they got there.

"There's one thing you have to open your mind to, Kierian," Sarah said.

"What's that?"

"Marconi isn't working alone."

"We already know that. He isn't here in Canada yet orchestrated the well-planned attack on you two tonight. He has a multitude of employees scattered all over the world."

"I don't mean that."

"What do you mean?"

"He's working with someone very high up in the mafia or the government in Italy. Or both. Whoever runs things over there has Marconi in their pocket, or he has them in his."

"What makes you say that?"

"Because an agenda is coming together."

"What agenda?"

"You said a Green Party member has information. An investigative reporter has stumbled onto something."

"Yes."

"The driver of the car we were in tonight told us to watch what we eat. What could that possibly mean? And could it be connected to the Green Party? Let me just say something's brewing, and it's deeper than we know or than your files on Marconi will tell you. At least that's my opinion."

They all got up and started for the door.

"Think on these things," Sarah added.

"I will," Kierian said.

"What hotel are we going to?"

"One near the airport. It'll be hard to track us with so many hotels in the area. No one would be able to locate us too easily. We'll get two rooms adjoining—"

"I think not. Put us on a different floor."

"That's not tactically sound."

"It's the sound part I'm worried about. I don't want you hearing us all night."

Sarah slipped her hand into Aaron's as they headed for Kierian's car.

"Sarah, you have to get some sleep."

"I'll sleep on the plane. This is my last night with Aaron until I fly back from Europe. I'm going to lick his wounds."

"Too much information."

"Just drive fast."

Chapter 4

THEY AGREED TO MEET at Kierian's car at ten in the morning.

Five minutes late, Sarah exited the hotel's sliding doors and stepped into the morning sun with Aaron behind her. She felt the heat on her skin immediately.

"You're late," Kierian said.

"We're not that late," Aaron said. "We were busy."

They stopped at the side of the car.

"Aaron, I need you to do something for me," Kierian said.

Aaron shielded his eyes from the sun. "What is it?"

"Take my car and drive back home or wherever you're going this morning. I'll come back for my car when we return from Italy."

"You said that last night."

"How are we getting to the airport?" Sarah asked.

"Shuttle bus, courtesy of the hotel."

She shrugged. "Sounds good."

Kierian handed Aaron the keys. "I need you to take this, too." He pulled his weapon out. "Because I bought our new plane tickets last night, the paperwork won't be completed in time to take this with me. We'll get new weapons once we're in Rome."

Aaron took the gun and slipped it into his pants, covering it with his shirt.

Sarah looked around, but no one was watching them.

"Yours too, Sarah," Kierian added.

Sarah grunted but removed the Magnum and gave it to Aaron.

"Now go," Kierian said. "Stay out of trouble and stay low. Watch your back."

"Are you worried about me?" Aaron asked, a wide sarcastic smile on his face.

"I'm selfish. If something happened to you, I would lose her." Kierian pointed at Sarah. "So stay safe until we get back."

Kierian moved a few feet away to give them privacy.

"We've got five minutes. Say your goodbyes fast."

Sarah wrapped her arms around Aaron. "Take care of yourself."

"I will."

"I'm serious. These guys are animals. If something happened to you, I would never forgive myself."

"Nothing's going to happen to me, Sarah." He hugged her tight.

"I will smack your corpse if I come back to find you dead."

"Don't talk like that," he whispered in her ear. "We both

know that strength comes from a place of pain. You don't have to worry about me dying. I'm young, fit, and security minded."

She pulled away. "That's what I'm worried about."

They kissed long and hard.

"Sarah …" Kierian said behind them.

Aaron moved away. "You gotta go."

"I know. Be well. Stay safe."

Aaron let go of her and opened Kierian's car door.

"Oh wait, Aaron. Here, take this." He handed him a cell phone. "A pay-as-you-go phone. There's fifty bucks on it." He took another phone out of his jacket pocket. "The number to my cell is set on speed dial. Call this number if anything happens from when you drive away until we return from Europe. You'll get me or Sarah. There's one other number programmed in your phone. Only call that in an extreme emergency. That's my office. They won't talk to you unless it's life and death. Understand?"

Aaron examined the phone. "Yeah, I got it. You know, Kierian, you're all right."

Kierian slapped Aaron on the shoulder. "Thanks. Now stay safe. Godspeed."

Aaron got in the Impala, started it up, and pulled out of the parking spot. As he passed Sarah, she was sure he was crying.

"Bye, baby," she whispered.

Sarah had showered that morning and dressed in the same clothes as yesterday. Kierian already had a passport for her, and he would supply all the money she would need. They would shop once they arrived and get new clothes. She didn't need anything as they took the shuttle bus to the airport.

Their tickets waited for them at the KLM Dutch Airlines counter.

"Have you heard from Vivian lately?" Kierian asked as they walked through Toronto's vast airport.

"Last night. It was a note about the attack, but I didn't see it until the attackers were banging on the apartment door."

"Why not?"

"Long story. Let's just get to Italy, deal with what needs to be done, and then I'm coming home."

Kierian followed her toward the security gates.

"That's the plan."

Without interruption, they got through security, found their gate, and took a seat by the window overlooking their plane.

"I'm curious about something." Sarah crossed her legs and watched a family of four walk by, all wearing backpacks. "Why us?"

Kierian turned to look at her. "What do you mean?"

She met his gaze. "You do know something isn't right, right?"

"No, actually, I don't. What are you talking about?"

"If four FBI agents went to Italy and came home in a body bag, why are they sending only one—you and a civilian? What does anyone expect of me?"

"We haven't had time to talk. We were supposed to be on a flight in ten days. At that time, we would've talked more. Marconi's file is in my office. I was hoping you could read through it. But now that we're leaving right away, all that's out the window. After what happened last night, I can't go back to my office."

"You still didn't answer my question. All you said was why I didn't know the answer. Since we've got time to kill, tell me why us and why not a larger team."

Kierian cleared his throat and looked around at the people gathering by their gate. After a minute, he turned to Sarah and lowered his voice. "We're going in under the radar. When the four men went previously, it was an official visit. No one knows that you and I are coming."

That doesn't sound good. "No one knows, eh?"

He shook his head.

"Then how did Marconi know?"

He shrugged. "I have zero idea."

"What are we supposed to do in Rome? I don't speak Italian. I don't know the city or the people. For all I know, I could end up in an Italian jail rotting away because no one *knew* I was there."

"Not going to happen. I'll know you're there."

"And what if something happens to you?"

"Don't say that. Nothing is going to happen to me."

She decided to change her line of questioning. "Who employs you?"

"What do you mean?" He chuckled. "The FBI."

"No, a name. Who is your boss? You know, in case something happens, and I need a contact."

Kierian was clearly perplexed. His face hardened, and he looked away, his hands fidgeting.

"What's the problem?" She uncrossed her legs and leaned forward. "I need more than just you and me. If you're my only lifeline, then who do I call if you're gone?"

"Look, Sarah." He twisted in his seat to face her. "It goes

deeper than offering you a name. This is supposed to be so far off the radar that no one knows anything. By isolating you, I'm protecting you. You're going to have to trust me on that."

The trip to Italy looked a lot grimmer.

Why am I doing this again?

"You're not inspiring me to go," she said.

"I know, and I'm sorry. But I need you. You're the only hope we have."

"And why's that?"

"Because you have an ability that almost guarantees you stay alive."

She leaned back and rubbed her chin. "Interesting way to look at it."

"That's how I see it. You think you're answering prophecies from your deceased sister and saving people's lives, which you are, but you're also saving your own. You should have died at the hands of that gang leader back in Toronto. Or the Leap Year Killer who snatched you from them. You're constantly put in the hands of the worst human beings, and you have a unique ability to stay alive." He cleared his throat again. "That's the kind of person we need in Italy. Marconi is a difficult man to stop."

"Is that all I'm going to get out of you—more about me?"

"For now."

Kierian looked anxious. Something was bothering him as he scanned the people gathering by the gate. He checked his watch, got up, and stared out the large windows onto the tarmac where the planes parked at their gates.

Their talk must have bothered him.

She shut her eyes and leaned her head back. Before her cousin Russell, who also had a psychic talent, had died, he left her a letter. In it, he told her to take this deal and go to Italy, or she would be dead before April 22, her birthday. When Kierian presented the idea, she had agreed instantly, but everything about this deal bothered her.

If it weren't for Russell's letter, she would not be going to Italy with as little information as she had.

It almost felt like she was going to her death instead of leaving to avoid it.

The cell phone in Kierian's jacket rang. Sarah popped her eyes open and got up. Kierian pulled the phone out.

Is Aaron in trouble?

"Who could that be?" she asked.

"I only gave this number to Aaron." He hit the answer button. "Hello." A pause. "Okay, Aaron. Calm down."

Sarah reached her hand out to take the phone, her stomach churning.

"I understand—just tell them the truth."

"Give me the phone," Sarah said.

"Here, talk to Sarah."

She grabbed the phone as Kierian turned back to the windows as if he was searching for something.

"Aaron, what's going on?" Sarah stepped away from Kierian and the strangers on the seats along the row she stood by.

"I don't know what to do," he said. "I'm a block from my building. The entire place is surrounded by emergency vehicles."

"And you think this is related to last night?"

"The odds are pretty high. The side road a few blocks up

from my building where you and Kierian shot that guy last night is completely blocked off."

"Can you go somewhere until they all leave? Remember, as far as the police know, this was some kind of movie scene."

"Who knows if that was true."

"Yeah, but those men were definitely shooting blanks." She turned to Kierian, who was still staring out the window as if searching for something. He was on the balls of his feet now, twisting his head back and forth.

"Or they were just trying to miss," Aaron said.

"Either way, you can't go home right now. Can they see you?"

"No, I'm far enough back that even the guys managing the roadblock can't see me."

"A roadblock? That's serious."

"It's probably set up to keep the area secure while they investigate."

"Aaron, give me a second." She walked over to Kierian. "Everything okay? You look concerned about something?"

He shook his head. "Just looking for our plane."

"That's it." She pointed. "The big KLM jet parked at our gate."

"Just finish with Aaron. Then we have to talk about something else."

"Okay." She turned away from him and stared out the window. "Aaron, could the roadblock be there to watch for the suspects and—" she stopped talking as a thought struck her. "Oh shit, Aaron."

"What?"

"The guy was shot by two different weapons last night."

"So?"

"Both those weapons are in the car with you. You could be in serious trouble if they pull you over or find out it originated in your apartment."

"You're right. Time to leave." The engine revved through the phone. "They will know it's my apartment by now. Mine's the only one with the busted door. It's probably still sitting wide open."

"What are you doing now?" She snuck a glance at Kierian, who checked his watch.

"I'm doing a U-turn—oh, no."

"What?" Sarah's stomach filled with acid. She needed to sit down.

"One of the roadblock cops just turned my way. Dammit, now he's pointing at me."

"Aaron, get out of there."

"I'm trying, I'm trying, but another car has decided to do a three-point turn in front of me. I can't move."

Sarah walked ten feet down the windows and sat on the carpeted floor by the gate's door.

"Talk to me, Aaron. What's going on?"

"You're not going to like what I have to say." His voice turned somber, defeated.

"Aaron?" A tear formed in her eye. She wiped at it. "Please tell me you're okay." She pushed her head into the glass behind her.

"It'll be okay, Sarah."

"What'll be okay? Tell me what's happening."

"Three police cars just came around the corner up ahead. They're stopping traffic from leaving."

"Do you think they'll stop you?"

"Sarah, six officers just got out of their vehicles. They're headed this way. They're staring at me through the windshield. It's weird … like they knew I was coming or knew the car."

She looked at Kierian, who moved to the aisle and watched the long walkway that led back to the security check-in area.

What could possibly be wrong with Kierian?

"That's impossible," Sarah said. "You're in an FBI-registered vehicle. No one would know it was you."

"Sarah, I'm going to put the phone on the dash. Just listen from here on in."

"No, Aaron, wait." But it was too late. The phone made a clunking sound as Aaron set it down.

Sarah got to her feet and started toward Kierian, the phone pressed hard into her ear. Through the phone, someone shouted for Aaron to get out of the car.

"What's going on, Officer?" Aaron asked.

"Step out of the car, now. Keep your hands where I can see them."

"Shit, Sarah, if you can still hear me, they've got their guns out now. Okay, Officer, I'm opening the door. I will get out."

Sarah had almost reached Kierian. "Aaron, don't. What if they're more men from last night?"

But he couldn't hear her.

"Hands up!" someone shouted.

"They are," Aaron shouted back. "Sarah, I'm scared. These cops aren't acting normal. I'm getting out now," he shouted. "Sarah, if you can still hear this, tell Kierian I'm probably going to need a lawyer—"

"I said hands up!"

A gun fired.

"No," Aaron screamed.

"Aaron," Sarah shouted into the phone.

"Sar—" Aaron's voice was cut off by gunfire. Then the phone died.

Tears streamed down Sarah's face as she looked at the dead phone in her hand. Eyes wide, on the edge of a panic attack, she looked at Kierian. His face was a wash of fear and embarrassment.

"Sarah, keep calm. Everyone's watching us."

"Kierian, call Aaron back," she stammered. "They were shooting at him."

"Look, Sarah," he started, but someone shouting cut him off.

Down the center of the airport's walkway, at least six armed police officers ran their way.

"It's time to leave," Kierian said.

"What?" Sarah said. "What's going on?"

He grabbed her arm, but she yanked away.

"What the hell is going on?" Sarah asked again. "I'm not going anywhere with you until you tell me what's going on."

"We have less than thirty seconds before those guys get here. There's no time to talk. Are you with me, or do you want to die in custody?"

Sarah looked back at the approaching authorities. Then turned to Kierian. Aaron came to mind at that moment, and she remembered Russell's letter. She hated cops, but Russell said she had to go to Italy. Her decision was already made.

"I'm with you," she said.

"Toss the stupid phone, and let's go."

She threw the phone aside and followed Kierian to the gate's doors. He opened them, and a security alarm blared. People recoiled at the noise and stepped away from the doors.

They ran down a tunnel to the left of the one where their plane was parked and came to the open square door. Without hesitating, Kierian bent down, grabbed the edge, and flipped over the side until he was dangling by his hands. Then he let go and dropped to the tarmac. Sarah did the same.

Once on the tarmac, he turned to get his bearings. Then he pointed. "That way."

Pulling to a stop behind the large KLM jet was a small Learjet with United States official markings and an American flag decal by the pilot's window.

She wasn't impressed by Kierian's show of power. All she could think about was Aaron. Was he okay? Did the Toronto police just execute him?

The side door of the jet opened, and a small stairwell lowered to the tarmac just as someone yelled from the walkway behind them.

Kierian hit the stairs first, made sure Sarah got on without incident, then jumped up and ducked inside himself.

"They're in," a woman shouted as she yanked on the stairs and closed the door.

The plane's engines revved, and it moved almost immediately.

Sarah leaned on the backrest of a chair, trying to catch her breath, her ribs protesting where they had been injured weeks before.

"What … the hell … was that?" she asked.

Kierian had flopped down in a chair and was watching

the terminal through the window. "Must be your fake passport." He looked at her, his face a deep red. "Their computers must've caught on."

"What fake passport? I thought you had my real one. I gave it to you."

He shook his head. "I couldn't allow anyone to know you were coming. I had a fake one made for you, but it was a rush job. I'm amazed it got us through security."

"You're not serious?"

"At this point, according to anyone who checks any flight records, an American named Sarah Roberts is not on any flight leaving Toronto and will not be. She has gone missing since," he checked his watch, "five minutes ago." He looked up at her. "My colleague at the bureau will call it in."

She took a seat opposite him. Something about his plan sounded good. "Tell me why?"

"You're off the map, off the radar. This way, no one can find you or know where you are. You're the safest you've ever been."

"What about Aaron? What I heard on the phone wasn't good. We have to do something."

"And we will." He raised a hand and called the woman who let them in. "Sheila, find out what happened to Aaron. He was driving my car a block from his apartment building when the police stopped him."

She nodded and walked past them, making her way to the back of the plane.

Kierian reached over and tapped Sarah's hand. "It'll be okay. Trust me. I've got everything under control."

He laid his head back and closed his eyes.

She did the same, her thoughts on Aaron. There was

nothing worse than involving loved ones in her tangled life. She had learned that lesson when her parents were kidnapped all those years ago.

One of the pilots spoke into his radio about clearance for takeoff. He mentioned the tail number or some other number, and the plane shot forward.

Could it be possible Aaron escaped numerous attempts on his life by hardened criminals only to be shot by the Toronto Police?

She refused to believe it. He had to be okay. He wouldn't have gotten out of the car with a weapon in his hand. There would be no provocation to shoot.

So why would they shoot?

The vibrations of the plane, combined with her lack of sleep the night before, acted like a sleeping pill.

She shot forward in her chair, wanting to be awake when news came of Aaron's safety.

But during the flight to Italy, all Sheila could gather was, according to the Toronto Police Department, they had not apprehended a man named Aaron Stevens.

In fact, no one knew that name at all.

Chapter 5

THEY LANDED IN ITALY to comfortable spring weather. It was already quite warm and sunny in Rome, with no clouds in the sky. The flight over had been smooth until they entered Italian airspace, where it got bumpier. Once they were cleared for landing, the plane taxied to a spot close to the terminal, and Sarah woke up Kierian. He had slept almost the entire way.

"The pilot had to file a flight plan," Kierian said at the door as they were about to deplane.

"And?"

"It got altered on the way over Amsterdam."

"What does that mean for us?" Sarah asked.

"According to Fiumicino Airport, we flew from a country inside the Eurozone—"

"Which means no immigration," Sarah finished for him.

He stepped down to the tarmac and faced her. "How did

you know that?"

"I was in Europe a few years ago. When traveling inside the Eurozone, it's like there are no borders."

They started toward the terminal.

"What part of Europe were you in?" Kierian asked.

"Budapest, Hungary. I ended up in Italy for a little while."

Kierian reared back. "So you've been here?"

"For a couple of days. Mostly a few hours' drive north of Rome. I didn't really get to enjoy it."

"Maybe this time things will be different."

They entered the terminal and started across the wide-open walkway that led to the front of the airport, where they would find a taxi.

"Isn't anyone meeting us?" Sarah asked.

"The original arrangements were for our flight in ten days. Since we sped things up, no one knows we're here yet."

Sarah stopped short of the exit doors. "So we're on our own? Completely?"

Kierian stopped alongside her and placed his hands on his hips. "Is that going to be a problem?"

"Kind of. What about weapons, money, lodging?"

"I've got that covered. Sheila has a man bringing us a weapon to the hotel in," he made an exaggerated display of checking his watch, "two hours." He placed his hand back on his hip. "Anything else?"

"Don't get cocky." She looked over his shoulder to watch the people behind her. "What about money? I have none. I need new clothes. I can't fight crime in the clothes I wore when running from those thugs in my apartment."

Kierian pulled a wad of cash out of his pocket. He

flipped off ten euro bills and handed them to her.

She examined them to discover they were all hundreds.

"A thousand euros? What does that work out to in American?"

"A thousand euros is currently about twelve hundred American dollars."

"Oh, okay, that's good." She stuffed the money in her pocket. "I guess that about covers it for now."

"Good. I'm glad you're happy."

Kierian opened the exit door and strode outside without caution. Not once did he check the people close to them or look for someone following them. He seemed too confident.

She examined the surrounding area. Only families coming and going on vacation, businessmen with briefcases talking on cell phones, and a mother scolding her child for walking too far from her.

"You coming?" Kierian asked from twenty feet away. "Or do you want to shop here? At the airport?"

Sarah didn't answer him. The door he had exited through remained open.

A man dressed in black pants and a black collared shirt leaned against a circular post. His eyes were hidden in the shadows of the brim of his cowboy hat. His hat and boots in an Italian airport stood out. He also appeared to be watching her.

She walked through the door and caught up to Kierian.

"Why'd you pause?" Kierian asked. "The fact that you're in Italy, the sunny peninsula? Are you already sightseeing?"

"You remember the driver we shot last night? Or whenever it was, with the six-hour time change."

Kierian waved at a taxi. "What about him?"

"He said we wouldn't last twenty-four hours in Italy and to watch what we eat."

"Oh, yeah, him. And?"

"I just thought I caught someone watching us." She looked back, but the door remained closed behind her.

"Impossible. No one knows we're here. Marconi isn't *that* powerful."

A taxi pulled up, and the driver got out to open their door.

Once they were seated, Sarah said, "What do you mean by that?"

"One second," Kierian said to her, his finger raised. The driver had said something in Italian that was unintelligible to her. Kierian leaned forward and said, "Per Termini, per favore."

"You know Italian?" Sarah said.

"A little."

The driver pulled away from the curb, jerked around a couple of parked vans and a bus that was backing up, jumped a speed bump, and turned up a ramp to exit the airport.

If the cowboy were watching them, he would have difficulty following them now.

"Wow, what's the hurry?" Sarah asked.

"This is Italy, Sarah. You'll get used to it."

"Not sure about that." The front windows were down, the wind creating a cacophony in the back seat. Sarah's eyes were tired and dry. She rubbed them and bumped Kierian's arm to get his attention.

"Are you concerned about the warning?"

He chuckled. "Of course I am." He leaned in close even though the driver couldn't hear them over the wind. "But no one knows we're here. Makes the threat useless. As far as anyone's concerned, you and I just dropped off the map. Last known location was Toronto. That's all they have."

She inhaled a deep breath. "What about Aaron? Is that why he's disappeared, too?"

"I thought Sheila told you what she found out on the plane."

"She did, which amounted to the Toronto Police knowing nothing about him, yet I was on the phone when they attacked him. There are a lot of puzzle pieces, and none of them are fitting. I don't even know what we're supposed to do here."

He tapped her leg in reassurance. She almost smacked his hand away.

"Don't worry," he said. "A good night's sleep, a change of clothes, a good Italian meal, and we'll sit down and go over everything I know about Marconi. We'll get a car, tour Rome for a week, and report back to the Hoover building what we've discovered. That's it. We'll fly home after that."

"Somehow, I don't think it'll be that easy."

They were on a two-lane highway leading into Rome. The driver answered his phone and spoke rapidly in Italian, gesturing with his hands while driving like a lunatic.

"This is normal?" Sarah asked as the driver swerved between cars.

Kierian nodded.

Sarah wished she didn't have to deal with Sam Marconi so she could enjoy Italy more. The food, the wine, and the historical sites. Maybe a tour of the Coliseum, the Fontana Di Trevi, or the Pantheon.

Maybe one day, she would return to Italy with Aaron.

Then they could enjoy it together.
As long as he was still alive.

Chapter 6

Aaron had been shot before. He was no stranger to the pain and physiotherapy involved in adjusting back to regular life and the difficulties involved with that. As a physical, athletic individual who teaches martial arts in his own studio, spending month after month in a wheelchair during his recovery a few years ago proved brutal after being shot by a British madman.

That was why when the authorities opened fire, he dove to the concrete, rolled halfway under Kierian's Impala, and covered his head. When the gunfire stopped, rough hands dragged him out from under the car. Cuffs were violently slapped on him, and he was manhandled to the back of a police cruiser.

Now, hours later, he had time to think and decide what to do. They had left him in a square holding cell. It was more like a little room with a bench along the back wall than a jail with bars. The door sported a small square viewing window, and the walls were bricks painted a light yellow.

They had allowed him to call a lawyer, but the officer who brought him to the phone had to dial for him, and the number had to be verified as a lawyer's office before the phone would be given to Aaron.

What if he had a brother for a lawyer and wanted to call him at home? What if his father was a lawyer?

It didn't make sense. None of his rights were being violated as far as he could tell, but something wasn't adding up.

Hang with Sarah for one week, and you'll never trust another cop.

Aaron's own experience with the authorities hadn't always been perfect. When his sister had gone missing, they were slow to act. When it really mattered, they hadn't been there for him.

A knock on the door jolted him. He sat up straight as the door opened. It was the same cop who let him use the phone.

"Your lawyer's here. Come on. Get up."

Aaron was escorted through the police station to a room with a rectangular table and a chair on either side. Michael Frederick, his lawyer, was seated at the table.

"Frederick," Aaron said.

"Stevens."

The door shut softly, the officer standing with his back to it.

"Can he hear us?" Aaron asked.

Frederick shook his head. "Not in here." He shuffled a few papers, a grim look on his face. Then he collected them into one pile, set them aside, and clasped his hands together.

"What?" Aaron asked. "What's going on here? I was attacked in my home last night. I barely got out alive. Then …"

Frederick shook his head.

Aaron tightened his fists and then loosened them. "Talk to me."

"They have a tight case."

"What case? What are you talking about?"

"Aaron, they're saying you killed a guy last night."

Aaron's stomach dropped. He felt instantly sick. Thoughts raced through his mind. He replayed the events from the previous evening. The attackers used blanks. Kierian shot the driver in the wrist. Sarah shot his hand. Then they left the scene.

He shook his head and looked down at his lap.

"They have the murder weapons," his lawyer said. "Apparently, there are two guns. They have the body. They even have your prints in the guy's car."

"What?" Aaron felt his life slipping away. Everything he had worked for and built was about to fall off a cliff and disappear. "That's impossible. You have to tell them. I didn't do it."

"Okay, Aaron. I believe you. We've worked together for seven years. I'm not a criminal lawyer, but I came down here because I knew you needed a friend when you called. I can recommend a criminal lawyer for you, a good one. This guy will take everything they have and rip it apart. He takes the best T-bone they serve and hands it back to them, looking like hamburger. Trust me, this guy is good. Expensive, but good."

Aaron nodded, his eyes watering, mind racing. What

would Sarah think? What would life look like from behind bars?

"I didn't kill anybody," Aaron whispered, his lip quivering. He cleared his throat and wiped his face.

Gotta keep it together.

"Tell me what happened. Give me all the little details. I'll bring the new lawyer up to speed before he gets here."

Aaron explained the attack on the apartment, running to the car, and Kierian's help in escaping the driver with the Magnum.

"Kierian works with the FBI in the States. You can verify everything I told you with him."

"Where is Agent Kierian now? Do you have a phone number?"

"I had a phone. They took it away from me." He nodded at the officer at the door. "The phone they took was set to Kierian's number and Kierian's boss's number."

"Where is he?"

Aaron hesitated. "He's in Italy."

"Italy?" Frederick sounded appalled. "This just happened last night. How did he get to Italy so fast?"

"He was booked on a flight this morning out of Toronto."

"You said Sarah was with you. Where's she?"

"With Kierian."

Frederick picked up his pen and tapped it against his hand. "So the only two people that could corroborate your story are in Europe?"

"Yes, but what I said was true."

"I know, but we need proof. That's what they've got, proof."

"What have they got?" He wiped his face.

"They have a dead body in the front seat of a car a few blocks from your building. Your apartment door was damaged and sitting ajar when they arrived. A witness said they saw you diving into a car as it tried to get away from you. The investigator's theory is that you ordered the driver a few blocks away, pulled over on a quiet street, and shot the driver twice in the wrist and hand." He shuffled papers, stopped on one, and read something. "They found your prints on the car seat and both guns in the Impala you drove when they picked you up."

"I can't fucking believe this. That was Kierian's Impala. The FBI guy. One of those guns was his, and the Magnum was the driver's. As I said, Kierian disarmed him by shooting his wrist."

Frederick piled the papers again. "Aaron, something hit the man in the side of the head. They're calling it blunt force trauma. Since your hands are considered lethal weapons, please don't tell me you hit him."

Aaron lowered his head. "He had held a loaded gun to my forehead and threatened to kill me several times. I was extremely angry." He looked up. "I hit him once to shut him up."

They sat in silence for a moment.

Frederick pushed his chair out and got to his feet.

"I'll call my guy, see what he can do."

"They said it was a movie production. They had a permit and everything. How could the police know so much so fast? How did they know it was me in the Impala this morning? I wasn't even near my building yet."

Frederick opened the file again. After flipping a few pages, he stopped and read something.

"Anonymous tip."

"Anonymous tip?"

"Apparently, someone called at five or six in the morning and said that you would be driving an Impala with both guns on you around the time they apprehended you." Frederick met Aaron's gaze. "Considering your history with the police force and what happened with your sister, not to mention your considerable talents as a martial artist, the order went out to use extreme caution when apprehending you. According to the arresting officers, you were armed and dangerous and willing to shoot if necessary."

"Holy shit. You've got to be kidding."

Frederick rested a hand on the doorknob. "They don't know you very well, do they?"

Aaron was stunned speechless.

"Don't worry. I'll get my guy to come to see you."

He opened the door.

"When can I go home?" Aaron asked.

Frederick turned back to him. "You have a bail hearing in the morning. I've been told that it'll be denied."

"What does that mean? How long will I have to be here?"

"Aaron, a man is dead. They have your prints and witnesses who will testify that you were there. They have two guns found in the car you were driving that sound like they'll match the bullets used on this guy's arm. The only people who can help you are in Europe."

"What are you saying?"

"They won't let you out until trial."

"And how long does that take?"

"Typically, a case like this goes to trial in a year or so."

"You're kidding," he burst out and slammed the table with his hands. "They can't just take my life away like that. I was attacked."

Frederick shut the door as the officer guarding it turned and touched the butt of his weapon.

"I understand, Aaron, but you're going to have to stay calm. If what you're saying is true, it'll all work out. Just give it time."

Aaron didn't know what else to say. He felt lost in a desert, everything a mirage.

Frederick moved back to the door, opened it, and walked out.

The officer escorted Aaron to be processed and placed into a different holding cell until his bail hearing in the morning.

The nightmare his life had become hinged on Sarah and Kierian coming home from Italy in one piece. With the testimony of an FBI agent, he was sure everything could be sorted out.

But who called in the anonymous tip? Who could know that he would be driving the Impala and have both guns on him when he didn't even know that would be the case until Kierian handed him the weapons and the keys to his car?

Unless it was Kierian himself.

Like a rigid puzzle piece, it all fit together.

Kierian had set this up. Kierian had called the police from the hotel before they met in the parking lot. It was Kierian's fault that Aaron was being arraigned on murder charges.

And now Kierian was alone with Sarah in Europe.

Chapter 7

"ARE YOU GOING TO say something?" Sarah asked.

Kierian hadn't seemed to notice the taxi driver's erratic behavior. "About what?"

She gestured to the driver and widened her eyes. "His driving."

The driver had stayed on his cell phone the entire ride into the city while he bobbed and weaved between the other cars. There were a few close moments when Sarah was sure they would be in an accident.

"Sarah, different cultures, different styles of driving. I've seen this before."

"Different cultures don't matter when your life is in jeopardy."

"But that's just it. Your life is not in jeopardy. He's an expert. Hasn't he delivered us to the heart of Rome without one fender bender?"

"That's not the point. If I spoke Italian, I would've said something. Although come to think about it, a slap upside the head translates into any language."

"Sarah, don't." Kierian waved a finger at her. "We're almost at the hotel."

She stared out the window. A large ornate church passed on the left. The streets were full, tourists already converging on the ancient city.

"How far will we be from the Coliseum?" she asked.

"This isn't a sightseeing trip."

"How far?"

After a moment, Kierian said, "A fifteen-minute walk."

The taxi slowed and stopped for a red light. Sarah took a deep breath and exhaled slowly.

"Has Aaron tried that cell phone again?"

Kierian shook his head.

"When we get settled, I want to call him myself."

"You can't."

She spun her head to face him. "Watch me."

"Sarah, we're here under the radar," Kierian whispered. "We can't be calling back home and giving up our hotel location."

The driver sped off when the light changed.

"Sounds reasonable. I'll use a pay phone somewhere."

"We'll talk more in the room." He smacked his leg. "Which reminds me. For obvious reasons, we're checking into the room as a married couple."

"What? When did this decision take place?"

He leaned closer along the back seat and spoke only loud enough for her to hear. "Sheila had new passports prepared in the plane. We're Mr. and Mrs. Cooper from Los Angeles. I couldn't tell you before because I didn't think Aaron would like it, and I didn't know the names until Sheila gave me the documents."

The taxi slowed again as traffic got jammed up ahead. A large sign on the building to the right said, Roma Termini.

"Is that the name you told the driver?"

Kierian nodded. He leaned forward and tapped the driver on the shoulder. "Qui va bene."

"What does that mean?" Sarah asked as Kierian dug in his wallet to pay the driver.

"I told him this was a good spot to drop us off."

After passing euros to the driver, Kierian got out on his side, and Sarah followed. The sun was dropping, and the fatigue of the twelve-hour flight weighed on her.

"Our hotel is two blocks that way," Kierian pointed. "Let's check in, get dinner, and wait for my contact to show. He's supposed to meet us at the room at," he checked his watch, "nine tonight."

Sarah followed Kierian through the mass of cars and Vespas. Hundreds of people came and went. It was too difficult to watch her back or to detect if someone was monitoring them. Kierian was a trained FBI agent, but he strode along the sidewalk without a care in the world as if a man with a weapon hadn't threatened them in Toronto last night.

A long line had formed by a bus with Terravision written on the side of it, the airport's name advertised on the top of the bus. Inside Termini, a long line of trains with aerodynamic noses waited.

A car door slammed behind them. She looked back for a quick second, then did a double take. The man dressed in black with the cowboy hat and boots moved away from the taxi and headed for the inside of the train terminal.

A horn blared. Sarah had stopped in the middle of the road to watch the cowboy.

"Sarah?" Kierian pleaded from the sidewalk. "Come on. Don't draw attention."

She headed his way but kept an eye on the cowboy. If he turned toward her just once …

She stopped beside Kierian as the vehicles she had held up drove past.

"What's got your attention?" he asked.

Without pointing, she said, "You see that guy with the cowboy hat and the black clothes?"

Kierian searched in the direction she was looking.

"He's about to use the escalators just inside the entrance to the terminal."

"Yeah, I see him."

"He was at the airport."

"Sarah, that's what people do. They fly in and then come to Termini to take a train to every part of Italy—"

She bolted. He called her name, but she kept running.

A man on a Vespa drove around a BMW and had to slam on his brakes to avoid hitting her. She hopped onto the sidewalk, dodged a group of teenagers with backpacks, and headed straight for the down escalator.

At the last second, the man in the cowboy hat turned around. He smiled and tipped his hat, and then disappeared from view.

Now he had to explain himself.

She hit the top of the escalator, jumped around three women, and ran down two steps at a time.

At the bottom, it opened up to a long hall with stores lining both sides.

The cowboy was nowhere in sight.

Kierian reached the top of the escalators and yelled something down at her.

What happened to 'don't draw attention to us'?

A small grocery store on her right seemed to have the most people. If she wanted to hide fast, that would be a good option.

She entered it and walked the first aisle. The store was set up so that she had to walk to the back of the store to turn down another aisle, where she found herself in the center of the store. The beer and wine were in the far corner, and the cashiers were to her right.

The cowboy had disappeared.

She checked two more aisles, walked through the checkout area, and moved back into the mall's main corridor.

Shit.

Kierian caught up with her. "What was that all about?"

"We're being followed."

Kierian grabbed her arm and guided her to the side. "Sarah, no one knows we're here. That's impossible."

She yanked her arm out of his grasp. "Grab me again at your own risk. I'm not your employee. I don't work for you, and you don't *ever* manhandle me. Clear?"

He stepped back. "Okay, sorry."

You don't sound sorry. "I know what I saw, and that man paid more attention to us than what is considered normal. Before he dropped out of sight, he tipped his hat at me."

"Maybe he thinks you're hot. The Italians are known to be a passionate people."

"He stood against a pillar at the airport and watched us leave. Whoever he is, he knows us."

"Okay, Sarah. Since we can't see him right now, can we go check in and get some food? Our contact is coming to meet us soon."

"See, someone does know we're here."

"Sarah …"

She grunted compliance and followed Kierian up the escalators. They crossed the busy street, the city almost dark as the sun's last rays died in the sky.

Half a block from Termini, Kierian entered a large door and took a flight of stairs to the hotel's lobby on the second floor.

"Buonasera," the man at the desk said. He looked like what Sarah would call a classic Italian. A Robert De Niro face with black hair slicked back.

"Buonasera," Kierian replied. "We're here for seven days. Sette giorni."

"Ahh, good Italiano," the man said in accented English. "Name-ah?"

"Mr. and Mrs. Cooper." Kierian smiled at Sarah. She didn't smile back. Not catching up with the cowboy and Kierian grabbing her arm only increased her irritability.

"I gotta you in a rooma twenty-seven. Here'sah you key, you TV remoteah and the airah conditioner unit controla." The clerk set everything on top of the counter. "Nowa, I just a needa you passaporta."

Kierian handed the man two American passports. Sarah took the opportunity to examine the exits and memorize the lobby.

"The passaporta information may take a few minutes,"

the clerk said. "Can you returno for them?"

"Certo," Kierian said. "Of course."

He started for the stairs with Sarah on his heels. Once inside their room, Sarah opened the balcony doors and stepped out to see how high they were and which direction the balcony faced.

She needed to go shopping. She needed a pad of paper and a pen. Vivian was probably aching to talk to her. There had to be something Sarah needed to know.

The balcony was small, and the air conditioner unit sat to the left of the doors, constricting the small space even more.

The street below was a narrow one-way with small cars lining both sides. To the left, it went as far as she could see, ending in a blur of trees. To the right, it stopped at the road where another Terravision bus was loading passengers bound for the airport. The train station walls rose behind the bus.

She looked toward the street at the corner and caught a glimpse of someone pulling back out of sight.

Someone wearing a cowboy hat.

Chapter 8

"TALK TO ME," SARAH demanded. "Tell me what you have on this Marconi guy while we wait for your weapon delivery guy."

"How about over dinner?" Kierian asked from the bed he had claimed as his. He was sprawled out, hands clasped behind his head.

"No. In the privacy of this room. I don't want anyone watching us or listening in."

"No one is watching us."

She tilted her head and glared at him.

"Okay," he said. "You saw what you saw. But, seriously, no one knows we're here."

"I disagree. Someone does, and they now know what room we're in. You know, for an FBI agent, you're taking this lightly."

Kierian frowned, but a second later, his face changed. He

jumped off the bed and ran to the balcony. She sat on her bed and waited. After a moment, he stepped back inside.

"I don't see anyone watching us."

Her gut warned her something wasn't right. How could the authorities in Toronto arrest Aaron as she heard on the phone and still no word? How could Kierian be such a good FBI agent that they authorized him to take her to Italy to hunt a man who had been killing high-ranking mafia bosses, and yet he acted like he was on holiday? She had not detected him acting as if he was in the line of duty since they had arrived.

Unless he's not here as an FBI agent ...

"What are we doing in Italy?"

Kierian walked to his bed and lay back. "Come on, Sarah, you've asked that question before. Don't break my balls. You know why we're here."

"Why aren't you acting like the tough, educated agent I met in Toronto while working that serial killer case with Detective Lyson?"

He opened one eye. "I'm the same guy. Maybe you've had a change of heart."

"Don't put this on me. You've changed, not me."

Someone knocked on the door. Kierian jumped up and ran over. Sarah entered the bathroom, which was behind the hotel room door, in case Kierian needed backup.

"Yeah?" Kierian said.

"It's me. Dinello."

Kierian smiled and whispered to Sarah, "My gun."

He opened the door and let a man enter. Then he checked the hall and shut and secured the door.

"Dinello, long time."

"I know, too long."

They embraced, then did a double kiss on the cheeks and slapped each other's arms.

"This is Sarah. She's here in an advisory capacity."

Dinello nodded at her.

They moved to Kierian's bed, where Dinello pulled a rectangular box out of his jacket.

"Kierian?" Sarah said. "While you two do this, I'll go back down to the front desk to get our passports."

"Okay, we won't be long."

Sarah left the room and walked the length of the hall to see where it led. Then she went the other way. Finally, she headed down to the small lobby. The same man sat behind the desk. He reached behind the counter and produced the documents when he saw her coming.

"Grazie." She picked them up off the counter.

"Prego," he said. "Buonanotte."

"Good night to you, too."

She headed up the stairs and knocked on their door. Kierian's voice came through the wood.

"Yeah?"

"It's me, Sarah."

The door clicked. As Sarah stepped inside, Dinello passed her on his way out.

"That was fast," she said.

"Just a drop-off," Kierian said as he shut the door. "Sarah, come look at this."

She set the passports on the small desk and moved to the end of Kierian's bed. A gorgeous Smith & Wesson sat in a red velvet box.

"Is that brand new?"

Kierian nodded.

"Nice, but without testing it on the range, using it a few times to get used to it …" Five boxes of ammunition sat on the bed beside the weapon. "Who are you going to war with?"

"Pick it up. Feel its weight, its beauty."

She wrapped her fingers around the handle and checked to see if it was loaded. Everything was crisp and clean as if it had come from the factory an hour ago.

After a thorough examination, Sarah set it back in the box.

"Where's mine?" she asked.

"That's a problem."

She flopped onto her bed, unsure she could stay awake any longer. "Why's that?" she asked, not willing to fight with him until tomorrow.

"Dinello was hired to bring one gun to the room upon our arrival. If we had stuck to the original plan and come to Italy in ten days, I would've arrived with my own weapon, and this one would've been yours. So he's coming tomorrow night with one more of these, same time."

Sarah closed her eyes.

"Fine," she whispered.

As she fell asleep, Vivian came to mind.

She was screaming for Sarah to get up and leave the room.

But Sarah fell asleep before she could listen to her.

Chapter 9

Something banged against the door, waking her with a start.

"What?" she mumbled and rubbed her eyes. She felt heavy with the time change and jet lag, her limbs difficult to lift.

"It's just me," Kierian said. He stood by the door, having just put his shoes on. "I'm going down to the lobby to check in with my superiors on their computer."

Sarah sat up on the edge of her bed. Their hotel room was dim, illuminated only by the bathroom light. "Yeah, I saw that computer when we got here. What time is it?"

"Around six in the morning."

She sat up straighter. "Really? I've been out all night?" She looked down at her clothes. "And I slept in these?"

"Looks that way," Kierian said. "I'll look up Toronto news when I'm down there to see if I can find anything on

Aaron, okay?"

His voice was soft. He sounded like he actually cared.

She nodded, her mind foggy and tired. She needed a shower and coffee to wake up.

She got up, showered, redressed, and opened the doors to the balcony, taking in the quiet street below and the fresh air on her face. She was awake now and ready to face their first full day in Italy.

The room's door opened, and Kierian entered.

"Anything on Aaron?" she asked as she stepped back into the room.

He pursed his lips and shook his head a few times. "Sorry."

"Anything new at your office?"

"What do you mean?"

You're not the same man I met in Toronto.

"When you checked in? Is there any news? Damn it, why are you so evasive? You want information from Vivian, but you're not forthcoming."

"Is this the normal Sarah, or did you wake up grumpy?"

"Fuck you, Kierian." She walked past him and opened the door. "I'm going for a walk."

"Where?" he asked.

She stopped and looked back. "I need a pad and paper. I need clothes. I want breakfast." She turned and started off. "There's no danger here. No one knows we're even in Italy, right? And I am not buying a bra and panties with you. It's seven in the morning. Shops are opening soon. See you in a while."

The door shut behind her.

In the lobby, she got on the computer and signed in to the

browser. She brought up Toronto news and looked for any mention of the attack on Aaron's building or Aaron's arrest but found nothing. Kierian was right. Either it didn't happen, or it wasn't newsworthy.

She left the hotel and walked across to Roma Termini. Inside the train station, she kept a close eye on her back. The cowboy was nowhere in sight.

She realized it was stupid to fall asleep last night without changing rooms or even hotels. If the cowboy worked for Marconi, they could've attacked them while they were sleeping.

A café was open to an abundance of tourists and Italians lining up for their morning espresso or cappuccino. Sarah got in line and used one of the hundred euro bills for her two-euro beverage and croissant to the clerk's chagrin. In English, she tried to explain that she needed a lot of change to use the pay phone. The clerk gave her almost twenty euros in coins, probably as payback for using such a large bill.

She drank the espresso at the counter and left the store, eating the croissant as she headed to the bank of pay phones along a far wall.

At the phones, she dialed the international code for the States and added Parkman's number from memory. Then she dropped euros into the slot until the call connected.

He answered on the second ring.

"Parkman," Sarah said, relieved. "I'm so happy you're there."

"Sarah! Long time. I'm the one who is happy you called. How are things?"

"I heard from my parents that you were back in Santa Rosa and working at your security firm full-time again."

"Someone's got to build this empire."

"Is there a toothpick in your mouth?" She looked around behind her. At this early hour, only half a dozen people milled around this part of the terminal.

"As always."

"Parkman, listen. I'm into something, and I'm not sure what's going on."

"What can I do to help?"

"I'm working with a man named Special Agent Penn Kierian of the FBI—"

"You're working with the feds? What the hell happened to the Sarah I knew?"

"I know, long story. When I get home, I'll fill you in. Anyway, there's something about him I don't trust. Can you pull some strings and see what you can find out?"

"I'll call in a favor. Come to think of it, there's an agent who owes me a huge favor from the days when they got the bust of that Mormon compound you liberated years ago. Jill Hanover. I'll call her. What's bothering you?"

"Listen, the phone may cut off at any time. I'm in Termini station in Rome on a pay phone, and I have to use coins to call."

"All right, just spit it all out. I'm writing everything down."

"Aaron called me. The Toronto police had surrounded his vehicle. There was gunfire, then the phone died. I haven't heard a thing. Can you find out if Aaron has been hurt, killed, or arrested? Also, get everything you can on Agent Kierian."

"That it?"

"Yeah. How long will this take?"

"Call me back in thirty minutes."

"Really?"

"Call me back. Whatever I have, I'll give to you."

"You're a prince."

"Do you need me to come to Italy?"

"No, I just need information for now. Then I'm coming back." A thought struck her. "Can you also look up Sam 'The Dealer' Marconi and give me the breakdown of who he is and what his agenda might be?"

"Consider it done. Call me back."

The line went dead.

Sarah set the phone down, longing for the old days when Parkman had her back. Without him, she would be dead right now. He had followed her to that FLDS compound all those years ago and saved her. Then he followed her to Europe and helped her hunt Armond Stuart, an international human trafficker.

She missed Parkman, but life had taken her in another direction.

The stores were opening in Termini. Within forty-five minutes, she completely changed her wardrobe and even bought a small wallet to hold the money Kierian had given her. After another espresso, she threw her old clothes in a waste basket and headed for the pay phones again.

The entire time, she looked for the cowboy but caught no sight of him or anyone else paying any kind of special attention to her.

At the phones, she dialed Parkman, her stomach turning at what he might have found out.

"Parkman here."

"It's Sarah."

"What do you want first, Kierian, Aaron, or Marconi?"

"Aaron."

"Nothing. At least, that's what you get at the first level. Then I called Detective Waller, retired. Remember him?"

"How could I forget the man who wanted to kill me?"

"He checked in with his old buddies and called me back. Aaron has been arrested for murder."

"What?" Sarah yelled. She looked around, having caught the attention of passersby. She hunkered in close to the phone. "How is that possible?"

"According to Waller, they have the car, the murder weapon, actually two murder weapons, and his prints in the deceased's car."

"But Aaron didn't murder anybody. I was there."

"Can you tell me about it?"

Sarah explained what happened the night she was warned against coming to Italy.

"And you still went?" Parkman asked. "Yeah, of course you did. Almost forgot who I was talking to."

"I have to get back to Toronto. I can clear it up. I was a witness. The guy was still breathing when we left, and it was Kierian and me who shot his wrist and hand, not Aaron."

"Speaking of Kierian, you want him next?"

"Shoot." Her stomach was in knots. Her fear of what Aaron was going through made her physically sick. It was all her fault for agreeing to come here. When this was over, Marconi would pay the ultimate price.

"There's only bad news when it comes to Kierian."

Her stomach dropped further. "What do you mean?"

She checked her back.

"There is no Special Agent Kierian who works for the FBI. Never was and isn't now."

Sarah was stunned speechless. How could Kierian have fooled Detective Lyson in Toronto for so long? How could he fool her?

With an authentic-looking badge.

"How accurate is this information?" she asked.

"One hundred percent. No doubt. Agent Hanover called all the way upstairs. The last thing she wants is to be responsible for you getting in trouble. I told her your life was at stake. She almost failed you twice. Trust me, she is absolutely sure there is no Agent Kierian anywhere in their system. Even if he's deep undercover, the system she looked into would at least have a name, but she found nothing."

"Then who does he work for?" she said, almost to herself.

"I thought the same thing, so I looked his name up. Nothing remotely matches what you gave me."

"When I get back, he will have a lot of explaining to do."

The pay phone timer warned her of a minute left.

"One sec, Parkman. I have to put more coins in the phone."

Once that was done, the timer showed three minutes, and she was out of coins.

"We have three minutes until it cuts off. I'm out of coins. But that's okay because I have a fake FBI agent to go kill."

"Sarah, be careful. You don't know who he is."

"What have you got on Marconi?"

"Too much for three minutes, but the highlights are, he's a hired assassin. The mafia has used him for over a dozen years. He's known around the world, like Carlos the Jackal. Serious player. If you're going after him, you can't do it alone. He has a team of mercenaries as security men."

"After I'm done with Kierian, or whoever he is, I won't be going after Marconi. This job sounds like it's over."

Unless it's Marconi who's fucking with Aaron.

"Recently, Marconi popped up in the news for claiming responsibility for the killing of a politician who was running for re-election, the minister of agriculture."

"How would the agriculture minister be in the same league as mafia dons?"

Sarah looked around, but still, no one seemed to be paying her any special attention.

"Don't know, but this guy is not someone you mess with. Even if you get lucky and kill a man like this, they have contingency plans in place, they have—"

The phone died.

"Shit."

She hung up. There was no time to get more change.

She had a man in a hotel room using the name Penn Kierian who needed to be hospitalized, but not until he explained who he really was.

Since no one knew they were in Italy, she could break a dozen of his bones, get on the Terravision bus outside the train station, and head to the airport, where she had enough cash to get on the next plane heading to Toronto before noon.

She would fly as Mrs. Cooper with the passport in the hotel room and get to Aaron's side within fifteen hours.

No wonder I don't trust the authorities.

She hit the escalators heading back up to the street level with the first real smile on her face in days.

This was the part she was going to enjoy.

Kierian had no idea the world of pain that was coming his way.

Chapter 10

At the street level, cars, Vespas, and buses were stopped, caught up in a massive traffic jam in front of the station. Even before nine in the morning, this area of Rome bustled.

She meandered through groups of people going every which way and got to the road where she sidestepped between two taxi cabs.

How could Kierian pull off that lie for so long?

Her anger grew with every step. Parkman was a trusted source, and Agent Hanover didn't just owe Parkman, she owed Sarah. There was no way the information could be wrong.

Kierian was a fraud.

Her anger almost boiled over when a tourist stopped in front of her talking animatedly on his cell phone about the police.

Instead of shoving him aside, she slowed to listen.

"Yes, I think the guy was murdered." The man stopped, turned to Sarah, who had edged closer, and frowned at her. He moved away, whispering into his cell about strange people.

Emergency vehicles blocked the side street her hotel was on, which caused the rush-hour-like conditions.

She pulled her hair together and rolled it into a bun, shoving the tip inside to secure it.

Then she moved toward the small crowd that had gathered at the police line. The twenty-four-hour warning from Marconi's men came to mind. Could this police response be for Kierian? Did someone attack their room?

Her anger, cooled by self-preservation, a sense of change if Kierian had been hit, made her falter. If it was Kierian, were they watching her right now?

She looked around, but everyone in close proximity was paying attention to the roped-off area. She edged closer, pushing by a few people to see down the street.

An ambulance was parked at the door to her hotel. Seven police cars lined the street around the ambulance in various states of parallel and double parking. Bumped by the crowd around her, she pushed to stay near the front.

A young couple with British accents talked quietly beside her about the murder. She tilted her head to listen better.

"A man was standing on the balcony, looking at the street below," the male Brit beside Sarah said. "Someone shouted something. The man on the balcony looked up. At that exact moment, he jerked his head back. Then he fell backward, out of sight."

"And you saw all this?" his companion asked.

Sarah maneuvered in front of the British man and

woman. "Which balcony?" Sarah asked.

The man, clearly shaken at what he had seen, his face pale, pointed up at the hotel. "The one that officer is standing on."

Sarah followed his finger and fixed her gaze on the balcony of the room she and Kierian had rented as Mr. and Mrs. Cooper. An Italian cop stood on the balcony, a man in a white crime lab coat on his hands and knees beside him. The cop was reading something he held in his hands.

Our passports.

A hush over the crowd grew momentarily as emergency personnel came out the front door. Two men wheeled a stretcher into view. The body and face were covered in a white sheet that was strapped down. It was the approximate size and shape of Kierian.

Moments ago, she wanted to kill him, but her anger had dissipated.

She would be dead if she didn't go out this morning.

Where's Vivian?

Kierian's murderer was close by. Whoever did this would still be in the area, looking for her. This wouldn't end until they found her.

The threat in Toronto was real.

If the killer or killers had entered the room at any point in search of her, they would know the name she was using.

That meant a commercial airliner was out of the question.

She fixed her gaze on the cop on the balcony to confirm what he was holding. The officer scanned the crowd below and then looked back at the document in his hand. His eyes turned to the crowd again.

He's looking for the woman in the passport.

A realization dawned on her. With her passport, even if she wanted to, she could never get on a plane. She couldn't leave the eurozone.

But the trains didn't need a passport to travel.

All she had was the money in her pocket.

The officer on the balcony continued to search the crowd below. His head swiveled back and forth. He shouted something to an officer on the ground, then continued his search. When he turned her way, she spun around, offering her back, slipped behind a few people, and pushed forward.

After she had gone past half a dozen people, she looked over her shoulder.

The cop on the balcony was staring at her.

"È lei," he shouted, pointing at her. "Tra la folla. Fermala. Sta scappando!"

Sarah ran, having no idea what the cop shouted other than it probably meant that he wanted her to stop. She bumped into people, knocked someone's shoulder, and almost spun out of control as she tripped over the edge of a piece of luggage dragged by an overloaded tourist.

At the street corner, the crowd lessened, giving her more options. The street was still jammed, but vehicles were starting to get through. She ran between two buses and turned to get lost in the train station.

On the far corner, she caught sight of the cowboy. He leaned against a wall, watching her escape.

Any other time, she would change direction and chase him down, but now she had no option but to clear the area. They had her fake passport. They had a dead body. There was a brand new Smith & Wesson in the room with only her prints on it, unless Kierian had touched it after she left.

Nothing looked good right now. She needed to get somewhere safe and clear her head. She needed to find out what had happened and what was happening.

She got across the street before the authorities at the front of her hotel fought through the crowd of people milling around the cordoned-off area.

Inside the train station, she ran along the tracks searching destinations for a city name she recognized.

Ancona, Firenze, Napoli, Perugia …

She stopped running.

Perugia. She had been to Perugia years ago with Parkman. She remembered that area well.

The train was leaving in three minutes.

Perfect.

None of the police had emerged through the large opening to the train station by the road where she had entered. But they weren't far behind.

She ran to a ticket machine. Conscious of her pursuers, she hit the British flag button that turned the language of the machine to English. Then she followed the steps needed to buy a ticket. The train's sign now said it was leaving in a minute.

She looked at the gaping door to the train station.

Over twenty uniformed officers entered the terminal.

She turned back to the machine, her breathing coming in ragged gasps as her ribs reacted to the pressure with protest.

She hit the buy ticket button, and it asked for a credit card.

There was no cash option. She looked up. At the top of the machine, it said it was a credit card machine only.

She had no time to redo the purchase.

She slinked away from the ticket unit and ran along the train to an open door, where she hopped on.

She took a seat beside a woman on the second-class coach. A moment before the doors closed and the train started moving, three more people got on, none of them police.

All three moved through her car, looking for a seat in the crowded train. As the last man passed her seat, he smiled down at her. She didn't smile back. He had dark skin, hair pulled back into a tiny ponytail but otherwise clean-cut, dressed in jeans and a tight T-shirt.

He sat far enough away not to bother her.

The doors shut, and the train pulled away from the station.

Only then did she relax. The cowboy had missed the train.

Not once did she see a cop peek in the windows. They had to think she was still in the station somewhere.

If a train employee walked the train car during the trip and asked to see her ticket to validate it and she didn't have one, they would kick her off at the next station. Then she would buy one at that station for the rest of the journey and get the next train to Perugia unless the ticket guy would sell her a ticket.

No one would know where to look for her or what train she had jumped on. Soon she would be three hours north of Rome.

Whether it was the police looking to question her or a madman looking to kill her, she would hide for a few days and then call Parkman for advice. He would know what to do.

It would all work out. She had done nothing wrong.
But neither had Aaron.

Chapter 11

THE MAN IN THE T-shirt and jeans pulled his cell phone out and dialed.

"I've got her," he said quietly in Italian.

"Has she been terminated? Tell me, Frank, can we move forward?"

"She is still employed."

"What? Why hasn't she been terminated?"

"I think the cowboy is going to be a problem."

He waited as the man on the other end of the phone paused to think. The train cleared Roma Termini and turned in a wide arc to head north out of Lazio province and into Umbria.

"What are you proposing?"

"Infiltration."

"Infiltration?"

"The services you're paying for are the minimums of my

expertise. I'm an infiltration expert."

"I know that. Your talents came highly recommended. That's why you are where you are. But every minute she's still employed is another minute of worry for me. The conference is less than a week away."

"I understand, but don't you think it's odd that she's on a train?"

"A train?" He fell silent.

Frank waited, watching out the large window.

Then his boss said, "Where is it headed?"

"To the green heart of Italy."

"Umbria? Why?" his boss stammered. "Does she know about the conference?"

"That's why she's not terminated."

"Has the cowboy made contact yet?"

"No. But he's been watching her. She chased him yesterday, but he got away."

Frank checked the passenger across from him to see if he was listening, but the young man had an iPhone in his hands and earplugs in his ears. The woman across the aisle from him was nodding her head as it grew heavy in sleep.

"Make sure the cowboy never speaks to her."

"That's part of the infiltration plan."

"What is this infiltration you keep talking about?"

"I will befriend her. I will get Sarah to trust me. I will tell her I'm an investigative reporter and offer her information. If the cowboy makes contact when I'm not around, she won't trust him. Already he's gone about it all wrong. She thinks he's got devious intentions. This'll be an easy task. Then her termination will be quiet, not loud and messy."

"You were hired because I understood you could handle

this task. If this is how you feel it needs to be dealt with, then so be it, but the timetable remains the same. Termination within six days. I will not attend that conference with her on Italian soil, only under it. Understood?"

Frank nodded, even though his boss couldn't see him. "Will The Dealer be brought up to speed in time?"

"I will handle The Dealer. That is not your concern."

Frank clicked off. It was his concern, but he wasn't about to debate that with the boss, a man of limited view. His employers never lived in his world, never walked in his shoes. They hired a hitman to execute someone, but they didn't know how much went into pulling the trigger or tightening the noose. How much planning went into making something look like an accident? How much planning went into pulling it off and being able to walk away? And not just walk away but remain on the outside of prison walls.

Sam "The Dealer" Marconi had managed to do that for many years. But now it was Frank De Luca's turn to be the most feared man in Italy.

And if their mutual political friend couldn't get The Dealer under control, then it would be left in Frank's hands to deal him out of the game.

There was nothing Frank De Luca wanted more, and the woman who could lead him to Sam Marconi was sitting on the same train, only a few seats up, completely unaware of the danger watching her.

He felt like a frog, watching a fly that was too close. A snake watching a mouse. A leopard examining a gazelle.

He smiled.

Sarah Roberts was his gazelle. Leopards were superior hunters in the wild, and Frank De Luca was a superior hunter in Italy.

The end was near. He dialed another number. After arranging a car to meet him in Perugia, he relaxed in his seat and waited the ride out.

Everything was going better than he could've planned it.

He smiled as the Italian countryside disappeared when the train entered a tunnel.

Chapter 12

As soon as the train went black and before the lights flicked on to illuminate the inside of the car, Sarah hopped up from her seat and made a beeline for the door that connected the train cars.

As she bounced through the door, the lights flickered on. She crossed between cars on a covered walkway and opened the door to the next one, which was just as full.

At the other end of the car, a man in a Trenitalia train uniform and cap had just entered. He turned to the people in the first set of seats to check their tickets.

She couldn't allow train officials to check her. She didn't have a ticket, and she'd be kicked off, but they would see her face and maybe call it in. They may even require a passport to give her a fine.

The least amount of official attention was the better way to go right now.

At the end of the next car, the train exited the tunnel, and sunlight poured in through the windows. She opened the next door, exited that car, and looked back over her shoulder.

It entered a tunnel again, but the lights were still on. A sign on the door beside her said toilette. She opened the door, entered the restroom, and set the lock.

She sat on the toilet lid and breathed a sigh of relief.

Chapter 13

As the train exited the second tunnel, Frank leaned over in his seat to look at Sarah.

Her seat was empty.

Merda!

He jumped up and almost collided with the Trenitalia employee checking tickets.

"Excuse me," Frank said in Italian and started to move away.

"Ticket, please."

Frank stopped. Sarah was still on the train. He would find her. They hadn't stopped yet.

"I almost missed the train in Termini. I didn't have time to buy one." He reached into his pocket and pulled out a few hundreds. "How much to Perugia from Termini?"

The employee sold him a ticket, validated it with a hole punch, and fined him fifty euros for getting on without a ticket.

The train entered another tunnel. He opened his mouth and clicked his jaw to clear his ears with the air pressure change.

He started the only way he was sure Sarah would've gone. She probably saw the ticket inspector coming and took off toward the front. She didn't get up and walk his way, or he would've seen her.

Frank had watched as Sarah tried to buy a ticket but stopped and ran for the train just before it left the terminal.

By being smart, patient, and observant, Frank believed in his skills as a tracker. Deduction alone allowed him to know which way she had gone.

They exited the tunnel. He had ridden this train many times. There were half a dozen tunnels, all just after leaving Rome. Soon the tunnels would stop. Soon the train would stop. And soon, he would find her and stop her.

In the second car, he traversed the seats, looking at everyone he passed, his smile wide as he pursued his prey.

This was the part of the game that he loved.

Chapter 14

WHILE SHE OCCUPIED THE restroom, she might as well use it. After pulling down her new pants, she sat on the seat.

The train car door just outside banged open as someone walked from car to car.

Must be the ticket guy.

After a few minutes, she would leave the bathroom and head the other way through the cars until she got to the end.

She decided to get off the train at the next stop, where she would buy a ticket to Perugia. There would probably be an hour's wait or longer for the next train, but that would give her time to eat and calm her nerves.

She stood, did up her pants, and cleaned her hands as best she could in the limited space.

The door banged outside the restroom again.

She waited and listened.

Without knowing where the ticket guy was, she decided

to wait a little longer.

Chapter 15

FRANK CONTINUED THROUGH THE third car without seeing Sarah. How could he have missed her? He had looked in every seat.

In the train station, as she ran along looking at the train destination signs, she had stopped at Perugia for a reason. He was sure that was her final destination.

He needed to remain calm. Just because he couldn't see her didn't mean things had changed. She was on a train bound for Perugia, and so was he. The train would make routine stops along the way, but he would watch to see if she exited at any of them and continue his pursuit from there.

At least until he could befriend her.

She wouldn't even know what hit her.

He entered the fourth car.

Still no sign of Sarah, and only two more cars to search.

Chapter 16

Sarah opened the restroom door slowly and peeked out. The compartment between the two train cars was empty.

She headed back the way she had come to avoid coming up behind the train employee. After walking through several second-class train cars, she came upon a door with a sign for first-class.

She stepped inside and looked the length of the car. It had better seats and was almost empty. She counted seven heads in a car that could hold fifty people. It had been the opposite in second class. There had only been seven empty seats and almost fifty people per car behind her.

In first class, each set of seats had a foldout table between them.

She passed a man on his iPad, a pie chart on the screen. Up ahead, a couple sat discussing a church they had just toured. At their chairs, the man looked up and tilted his head sideways.

Sarah went on guard instantly, her hands flexing at the first sign of a problem.

"Do I know you?" the man asked her in American English. He was dressed well in a suit jacket. His hair was combed to one side, and he had a thin goatee framing his jaw.

She shook her head and looked up the aisle to the end.

This is the last car.

She would have to head back the way she had come and chance bumping into the ticket man.

"Do you know when the next stop is coming?" Sarah asked.

The man nodded. "We'll be stopping in Terni within minutes. Where are you headed?"

"Terni," she said too fast.

The man narrowed his eyes. Keen eyes that took in everything. He had an iPad in his lap plugged into the train's wall. On the screen was a golf game he had been playing.

"Is it a lot more for first class?" she asked. "You get these tables and plugs to charge your devices."

"Not at all," the man said. "It works out to be about five to ten euros more per ticket. I do it because first class is hardly ever full, which makes it quieter, easier to read."

"Or play golf." She gestured at his iPad, then to the novel beside him. "What are you reading?" Sarah wanted to make conversation while she waited for the train to slow as it approached Terni.

"That's one of my books."

"Your book? Like, you wrote it?"

The man nodded.

"What's it called?"

"*The Drowning.* It's my new thriller."

"A writer, eh?" she said out loud, almost to herself.

He nodded, his eyes still observing her.

"I am, too," Sarah said. "I've written two full-length memoirs of my life. When I get home, I'll be working on my third."

"Where's home?" the man asked.

"Right now, Toronto, Canada."

"Me, too."

The train slowed.

"Well, I guess that's it," Sarah said. "Here comes my stop."

The man stood. Sarah reared back but realized there was no danger and made it look like the train's momentum caused her to lose her balance.

The man pulled out his wallet and handed her two business cards.

"When you get home, look me up on Amazon. I'm Jonas Saul."

"Jonas Saul. Why does that name ring a bell? Maybe I've read you before."

"Maybe," he said, his eyes never leaving her face.

"I'm Sarah Roberts." It was out before she could stop it. Advertising her name only left a trail.

The man stuck out his hand. "It's nice to meet you, Sarah. I knew I knew you from somewhere." He grinned like he'd just won a small victory. "Saw your name in the papers over the years. It's an honor to meet you. Keep up the good work."

The train was almost at the station. She had to go.

She clasped his hand, shook it hard, and let it fall.

They exchanged a smile.

"Gotta run," Sarah said and started away.

"Stay safe and run fast," Jonas said. Then he grinned, his eyes lighting up if that were possible. It was the kind of look she expected from an adoring father who was proud of his daughter and the decisions she had made.

Her step faltered.

What is it about this guy that draws me to him? Could he be that *friendly, or was there something else?*

She collected herself as the train stopped, nodded at him once more, and jogged for the door as she slipped the two business cards into her pocket.

"Say hello to your sister for me," he shouted after her. "And listen to her closely. Everything always depends on Vivian."

She stopped at the door and looked back, but Jonas was already sitting down.

She opened the train car door that led between the two cars and turned to leave through the open exit door on the side. A whistle blew. The door to the outside started to close.

She jammed her foot in it and forced it back open.

Then she slipped outside and dropped to the platform. The door closed behind her, and the train started moving almost instantly.

She moved away from the train and looked for Jonas but couldn't see him as the windows slipped by.

How does he know about Vivian?

Over the years, the Toronto papers had featured her many times. Three years ago, she was front page news after breaking into a religious compound and freeing female captives. Since then, she had been featured no less than a dozen times. Someone who watched the news routinely could easily recognize her, but it rarely happened.

She shook her head at the notion of familiarity and decided to forget about it. Jonas wasn't a threat. If anything, she'd felt comfortable in his presence.

The last train car lumbered by.

Inside, a face pushed up close to the window.

The smiling face of the man with the ponytail, T-shirt, and jeans.

Wow, some Italians have no restraint with the staring thing.

She turned around to buy a ticket, unable to get how Jonas made her feel out of her head.

Chapter 17

FRANK HAD GONE THROUGH the train cars all the way to the back. At the Terni station, he had waited at the exit door as long as he could, watching the length of the Trenitalia train for his prey, but Sarah did not get off.

To double-check, he leaned over the empty seats in the last car and stared out at the people walking toward the station as the train pulled away.

Once the train left Terni, he would walk back through it and check all the toilets. She had to be here somewhere.

But to his surprise, Sarah stood on the platform as if in a daze. She didn't move or react as he passed her.

He made sure to smile wide because they would meet again. He wanted her to remember his face.

They were going to be friends one day very soon.

After passing her, he took a seat and clenched his fist into his other hand.

There was nothing worse than being thwarted by an amateur. He was the tracker. He was the hunter. Yet she could elude him on the train for almost ten minutes and get off without him seeing her.

The mission would stay intact. Sarah was on the train to Perugia for a reason. Otherwise, she would've gotten on any train.

He would continue to Perugia and set up a meeting with Marconi while he waited for Sarah to arrive.

He was smart. He knew her. She was only in Terni to buy a ticket. Why else would she jump from her seat when the ticket inspector came through and then leave the train at the first stop?

She got off to buy a ticket to Perugia because that's where the conference was taking place in six days.

People were so easy to figure out.

Once this mission was over, he would kill Sarah as he was hired to do. No one got the drop on him and survived to talk about it.

At least not since the last guy was buried in three different parts of Italy.

No, Sarah Roberts would never go down for the murder of Sam "The Dealer" Marconi as planned. She would be dead before the authorities even got there.

The papers would come out the next morning with headline news about how the mafia don killer, Sam Marconi, was killed by Sarah Roberts, who then died in the explosion, too.

Such a tragedy ...

Chapter 18

Sarah bought her ticket, but the next train wasn't for another two hours. She bought lunch at a café down the street from the train station. Lunch consisted of some kind of uncooked ham on bread with tomatoes and a cappuccino. The sandwich tasted better than it looked.

Watch what you eat.

The warning from the driver in Toronto popped into her head. What could he mean by that? Was someone going to poison her?

Her thoughts turned to Kierian, and she paused to collect herself. He had been good to her. Stood up for her in Toronto a few times and lost his partner, Agent Tower Clint, to a gang of thugs.

But then Parkman told her that Kierian wasn't an FBI agent, and Parkman had it on good authority.

What would her continuing north accomplish? The

Italian authorities would be looking for her everywhere within hours.

Maybe she should just leave Italy on the train. Go to France or Spain. Buy a plane ticket there.

Not without a passport.

Maybe Parkman could get one for her. Or she could go to the American embassy and say she lost hers. But they'd probably turn her in to the Italian authorities.

She finished her sandwich, downed the cappuccino, and headed back to the train station. She would wait for the train on the fringe of the station, away from anyone else.

Once in Perugia, she would take a train to Umbertide, the city she stayed a night in with Parkman all those years ago. Maybe she could hide there for a few days, call Parkman, and work things out.

No one would expect her to be in Umbertide.

She paid for the lunch, and a business card tumbled out of her pocket. She picked it up and examined Jonas's face.

Before throwing the card away, she memorized his name because having it on her was a risk to Jonas.

Once back in Toronto, she would look him up and read one of his books.

Even though she didn't recognize him, an uncanny familiarity with that guy drove her crazy.

Maybe they would meet again one day.

She thought of Vivian and her silence since Sarah had run from Aaron's apartment.

On the way to the train station, she stopped at a store and bought a small pad of paper and two pens.

Come on, Vivian. Talk to me ...

Chapter 19

DURING THE TRAIN RIDE north into Umbria, she sat alone and examined the mess she was in. She had come to Italy with Kierian to gather intel on Marconi. But Kierian was a fraud, and now he was dead. Who had he been working for? Himself? Could Marconi know that?

She had to get settled, find an internet café, and learn more about Marconi. Kierian conveniently never got around to giving her Marconi's file or telling her much about him.

Maybe Kierian worked for Marconi. But if that was the case, why bring Sarah all the way to Italy? The authorities in Toronto knew of her relationship with Kierian. Questions would be asked unless this was planned as a one-way trip for Kierian.

The train employee came by her seat and checked her ticket. He punched a hole in it and moved on.

Her first priority was to get Parkman working on a secure

exit for her. She needed to clear her name with the Italian authorities, and Parkman was going to be pissed that she ran, but Kierian's killer had probably been watching.

It was always better to analyze her options outside of prison and to work out who was responsible for screwing with her.

Maybe that was their goal. To get her in jail and away from the pursuit. If so, was something coming up that would attract her attention? Something where Marconi was sure to attend and either kill Kierian and her or have them jailed, removed as threats?

With not a single thread of evidence of who these people were and no leads of where to go, she felt swept out to sea in a rubber dingy that was leaking air.

A name, Marconi, and a man dressed as a cowboy were all there was to work with.

She was sure as the air she breathed, the cowboy would pop up again, and then she could get some answers.

If Marconi could be nailed down, she would locate him, too.

Vivian, you could help, you know.

She laid her head back in the seat and watched the Italian countryside race by. They were coming up to a place called Assisi, which was a few stops from Perugia.

The late afternoon sun blazed through the window and warmed her.

At that moment, she missed Aaron more than ever before. She was truly alone.

Chapter 20

De Luca got off the train in Perugia and located the car waiting for him on the other side of the building.

"Don't drive anywhere," he said to the driver in Italian as he got in the back seat. "Stay in this parking area. Just move into a back corner spot and leave it running."

The driver did as he was told.

Frank opened the laptop waiting in the back seat for him. He signed in, attached the chiavetta to the USB port on the side, and brought the computer online.

In the browser, he typed Sarah Roberts and scanned the hundreds of websites that featured her. There were too many for what he was looking for.

He refined his search to Sarah-Roberts-Italy and discovered that she had spent time in Umbria roughly three years ago working an illegal immigration case with the Americans.

She had been part of a team that attacked a hideout in a crypt in Montone, right outside a small city called Umbertide, where according to the article, she had stayed a night in the Hotel Rio before leaving for parts unknown.

He leaned back in his seat and smiled. People were predictable. He knew people, and he knew Sarah. She wasn't heading to Perugia. That was just where the train connected and would take her to Umbertide. She was going to what was familiar.

When she realized her partner Kierian was dead, she ran. Where else would she go but to somewhere familiar? She's afraid and alone. Familiar comforts and soothes the wounded.

He constantly surprised himself at how good he was getting at this job.

"Guida," he ordered. *Drive.*

"Dove?" *Where?*

"Umbertide."

The car pulled away from the parking lot and dropped down from the city center.

His cell phone rang.

"Pronto?" *Hello.*

"Has our subject been terminated?"

Frank almost hung the phone up and tossed it against the window. It was people like his employer that annoyed him. Everyone else remained inconsequential in his life, but in order to enjoy the life he lived, people like his employer were a necessary distraction.

"She has not been terminated."

A gasp on the other end of the line. "I'm not understanding what's happening here."

"You will. Within two days, all that you've employed me

to do will be done."

"Even The Dealer?"

"Even him."

"You came highly recommended."

"Assure yourself with that. Don't allow doubts to enter your thoughts."

"Can you at least tell me where she is?"

"Umbertide."

"What? That's ridiculous. The conference is less than a week away. Of all places, she can't be there. Why is she there? We have to do something—"

"Shhh," Frank whispered and then waited for his employer to calm down. "Everything is under control. I will be in Umbertide in half an hour. I will meet her train. Within forty-eight hours, you will be assured of my success."

"Okay, okay … uhm, thank you."

The phone died.

Frank tossed it beside him and decided to limit the calls from the employer, whose doubts only served to bother and irritate him.

If it continued, there would be no good recommendation coming from this employer. Maybe the world would be a better place with this whining, sniveling bastard gone.

Frank closed the laptop on his thighs and made the decision.

When this was all over, and the payment for his services had been transferred to his account, he would make an unannounced visit to his employer and give him a free ride to wherever it was dead people went.

Chapter 21

SARAH SNAPPED AWAKE AS the train slowed at a station.

How could I fall asleep?

She did not want to sleep. Or was it Vivian who put me out?

The sign outside her window said Perugia Ponte San Giovanni.

She jumped out of her seat just as the train came to a full stop. After she got off, the train blocked traffic to the small terminal. The train took another couple of minutes to pull away so the people could cross the tracks and head inside.

A few dozen people waited on benches and stood around talking by the train building. This station seemed to be a conduit for many destinations.

At the Trenitalia ticket counter inside, the man behind the glass booth said tickets to Umbertide were bought at the café bar on the other side of the building. Trenitalia was a countrywide train. The one that went to Umbertide was a regional train.

She had to go outside to walk around to the café bar. There, she paid a couple of euros for a one-way ticket to Umbertide on track five that was not leaving for another twenty minutes.

Outside, no one else was waiting at track five yet. She walked over to a tree for shade and leaned against it. A young couple, not much older than her, sat on a bench close to the tree. She thought they spoke English, but their hushed tones weren't loud enough to discern the language.

She pulled the blank paper she had bought at the store in Terni from her pocket and flipped through the pages to see if Vivian had written anything while she had been asleep.

"On the back," the man on the bench said.

Sarah stared for a prolonged moment at him, then turned the pad over and saw what Vivian had said.

They're safe ... go with them ...

She frowned, then folded the pad up and slipped it back into her pocket.

Okay, Vivian. I'm trusting you here.

"English?" she asked. "I don't speak a word of Italian, so it's nice to hear a little English. I'm Sarah Robertson." She added the suffix at the last second.

"My name is Darwin, and this is my wife, Rosina," the man said as he extended his hand.

After they shook hands, Rosina did the same.

"On vacation?" Sarah asked.

They exchanged a glance. "Kind of," Rosina said. "How about you?"

You sure about this, Vivian?

"No, not a vacation. I'm running from the police and mobster-killing hitmen." She smiled as wide as she could, hoping the truth would appear as fantastical as it sounded.

The couple looked at each other again; concern creased their faces this time.

"You two know sarcasm, right?"

"Yes, yes, of course. Just, it, well, we've had a few bad experiences in the past."

"Really? That doesn't sound good." Sarah moved closer to the bench. "Where are you from?"

"Toronto," Darwin said. "Ever been there?"

Her eyes widened. "Yes, I just came from Toronto two days ago. Wow, what a coincidence. You're the second person from Toronto I've met on the same day."

"Seriously? You met someone else from Toronto today?"

"Yeah, a man named Jonas Saul."

Darwin frowned and looked down at the ground as if he was thinking. "Why do I know that name?"

"How long are you staying?" Rosina asked.

"Just a few days. Gotta get back."

"Here on business?" she asked.

Sarah looked down at her new clothes. "What makes you say that?"

"The only people who come to Italy for only a few days are here on business. Otherwise, you would stay for at least a week."

"That's pretty observant." She leaned on the back of their bench. "I'm waiting for the train to Umbertide. You too?"

"Yes, we live in that area."

"Must be nice."

"It is," Darwin said. "But what's really nice is to talk to a fellow Torontonian. It's been a long time. Sometimes we feel isolated out here."

The three of them looked at the train coming from the north.

"Is that our train?" Sarah asked.

"Looks that way," Darwin said.

They got up and headed to the tracks together, along with a small crowd from the train building.

"How long have you two been here?" Sarah asked.

Darwin put a comforting hand on Rosina's shoulder. "It's been too long," he said. "At first, we enjoyed the peace and quiet, but now that Bradley is here, we long for family and community."

"Bradley?"

"Our baby. He's at home with the nanny right now. We just went shopping at the Collestrada Mall here in Ponte."

The train arrived, and everyone got on. Darwin showed her how to use the small yellow machine near the doors to validate her ticket, and they took a seat together.

When they sat down, and the train got underway, Darwin and his wife whispered something to each other. Sarah gave them their privacy while she scanned for the cowboy.

Finally, Darwin nodded at Rosina and turned back to Sarah.

"Did I hear you right?" His face was stern, serious.

"Excuse me?"

"You said your name was Robertson, but I think it's Roberts. Aren't you Sarah Roberts?"

She looked around at the people close enough to hear, but no one noticed them. Vivian's message resonated through her head.

"Yes, that's my name." She leaned forward. "How would you know that?"

"We experienced a few problems of our own in Toronto." He looked at Rosina, the love in his eyes. Something Sarah longed to see again in Aaron's eyes. "Since we've been gone, I watch the news every day. I read them all: *City Pulse 24, The Toronto Sun, The Star*, you name it. Your picture and name have shown up often. I thought I recognized you."

"This is getting creepy. I'm on the other side of the ocean in Italy, and you're the second person who said they were from Toronto *and* that they recognized me."

"Who was the other one again?"

"That guy, Jonas. He was on another train."

Darwin snapped his fingers. "There's something about that name that rings a bell. It almost feels like everything bad that's ever happened to us was all his fault."

Chapter 22

FRANK HAD HIS DRIVER park on the road half a block up from the Umbertide train station, the car aimed to facilitate a fast exit if Sarah got suspicious when he approached her. He waited on the far side of the station. According to his calculations, the train she should be on was due in ten minutes.

Of course, she was coming to Umbertide. What better place to cool her heels than in a familiar location where the authorities would never think to look.

She could stay for weeks, even months, in any number of rooms or apartments throughout the city that were empty due to Italy's financial crisis. They had the second-worst economy in the eurozone, only beaten by Greece at the moment. Enter a city like Umbertide with cash, the people open their hearts and doors.

What Sarah wasn't counting on was her personal guide,

the lovely male specimen of Frank De Luca, who just happened to be waiting for her.

He wanted to warn her of a certain cowboy he had seen following her in Rome. He wanted to warn her of unsavory men who would only want one thing from her. He would befriend her, so she would join him for dinner in the back of a restaurant in the main piazza where Sam "The Dealer" Marconi would also be dining.

Murder would be the main course, with conspiracy for dessert.

Frank rubbed his hands together and waited for the train to show.

Seven minutes left.

Chapter 23

"Listen, Sarah, how would you like to join us for dinner?"

Sarah hesitated. Could she trust them? They had only met half an hour ago. If she could, should she go with them and put them at risk? They had their baby to consider.

Vivian's message was clear, though.

She nodded. "That sounds wonderful."

"Then this is our stop."

She looked out the window. "Pierantonio?" She looked back at them as they got up out of their seats. "I thought you said you live in Umbertide?"

"We do. But, as a precaution, we always buy a ticket to Umbertide and then get off one stop early. You never know who is waiting for you at your final destination."

She could really get to like this couple. "Good thinking." Her hand went numb, then tingled. Vivian's voice shouted in her head to go. "Your invite sounds terrific. I'd love to join you for dinner."

She followed them off the train and out to their car. The small four-door silver Fiat Panda looked no bigger than an enlarged golf cart.

As Darwin pulled out of the Pierantonio train station, Sarah realized this was the best idea in history. Whoever was searching for her would never know where to look. Vivian had given her blessing. Sarah was safe for now. Maybe she could stay the night, use their computer to do a little research, and get grounded.

Tomorrow would be another day. Tonight she would dine with Darwin, Rosina, and Bradley and forget about the world as it spun under her heels.

Although she knew that couldn't be true.

Aaron and what he must be going through were never far from her thoughts.

Chapter 24

THE TRAIN ARRIVED ON time. Frank walked closer to watch each person as they disembarked.

His cell phone rang. He almost didn't answer it, but it gave him an excuse to appear busy. He didn't want Sarah to think she was the only reason he was here. That could make her suspicious.

"Pronto?"

"I need results. I'm panicking here. What's going on?"

His employer. Frank committed to himself on the spot that he would never work with such a weak man again.

"I'm going to throw this cell phone away," Frank said.

The train came to a stop, and the doors opened.

"I need a plan. What are you going to do? I understood the female would be terminated this morning in Rome."

"Sometimes things change. I'm prepared. You have nothing to worry about."

The last passenger got off the train. The engineer looked at the length of the two train cars and got ready to leave.

Where's Sarah?

His employer was becoming a costly distraction.

"I'll decide what I have to worry about. I cannot have this female wandering around Umbria with so much riding on this conference—"

"And you won't." Frank turned away from the train as it started out of the station, heading toward Sansepolcro.

Where the hell is Sarah?

"Are you listening to me? You were hired for results. I was supposed to get those results this morning. They didn't come. What I want to know is—"

"You will get your fucking results." Frank moved away from the common areas so no one could hear him. The mission was slipping from his fingers. He had Sarah, and now she was gone.

"I don't need you in my ear," Frank continued, "constantly telling me what I was hired to do. I will finish what I started. I have never failed in a job. That is why I come so highly recommended."

"And highly-priced."

"If you're worried about the fee, deduct twenty percent for the delay."

"No, no, it's not that. I just need this finished so I can move on."

"Consider it finished, then. Move on now. You have my word."

"I don't want words. I want results—"

Frank slammed the phone down onto the concrete and crushed it under his boot. He kicked the broken plastic pieces across the ground, where they fell over the edge of the platform and onto the train tracks below.

It was time to clear his head, and he couldn't do that while listening to that whiny politician, nor could he allow his employer to continually call him for nothing.

He needed time to think about Sarah. Research her, learn what he could. He would examine her from afar and make educated decisions on what she would do and where she would go.

He had been so certain she would be on that train moments before he would have bet money on it. But she didn't turn up.

Losing his prey was not something Frank was used to. Could it be his prey was outthinking him? Was Sarah the first challenge he would encounter in the twelve years since he had gone professional?

He was beginning to even hate the sound of her name in his head. Nothing about her he liked made it easier to waste her when the time came.

But outwitting him would garner her a little respect. He couldn't allow it again. He would figure her out, and then he would destroy her.

The problem was time—there wasn't much of it.

If he didn't find her within forty-eight hours and get her to that dinner with Marconi, she would not be killed, but she would be killing him in the process.

His reputation as a professional would end with one stupid woman who bested him.

There was no way he could let that happen.

Chapter 25

Darwin pulled onto a long driveway lined with cypress trees.

"Italy has stunning landscapes," Sarah said.

Rosina turned in her seat. "Yes, it's peaceful here. Too peaceful, sometimes."

"Better than the alternative," Darwin said.

The alternative? Sarah wondered what he meant, specifically.

"What's your story?" Sarah asked as Darwin brought the car up to a double garage. "What brought you two all the way out here from Toronto?"

Darwin turned the car off and looked sideways at Rosina, who met his gaze. The tension in the air during that moment was laid on thicker than a blanket draping the three of them.

"I'm sorry," Sarah said. "Maybe it's none of my business."

"No, it's just a long story. A long, sad story."

"But one of triumph," Rosina said with a smile.

Sarah didn't see the smile in her eyes. Only pain.

"Come on in," Rosina said as she opened the car door. "The nanny should have the vegetables chopped by now and the pasta ready to be boiled."

Sarah followed them along a walkway with a row of shrubs on either side to an iron gate.

Darwin punched a code on a keypad, and the gate snapped open. A large German shepherd ran around the far wall of the house and lunged at Darwin. Sarah took a step back, the dog's animal power and fast actions making it look like it was attacking. Darwin handled the large dog well, grabbed his front paws, and let him lick his face.

"You're not much of an attack dog, Hercules, are you?"

Rosina laughed and walked around them. "Boys will be boys. Come on inside, Sarah. I'll pour some wine."

Dinner was served after the nanny left for the night. Bradley was put in his crib, and by eight in the evening, as the stars twinkled in the Italian sky, the three of them were sitting on the deck, sipping the digestivo grappa.

"Thank you so much," Sarah said. "That was an incredible meal."

Darwin set his glass down and looked up at the sky. "It's no trouble at all. Happy to do it." He looked like he had something else to say.

Earlier, before dinner, he had changed into a light-colored T-shirt. Below the lip of the sleeves, massive scars decorated his skin. It looked like skin grafts had covered up bullet holes. Either that or someone had torn a chunk out of each arm.

"We invited you here because we knew you weren't a threat through what I've read in the papers over the years."

Sarah nodded, waiting for him to continue speaking. Rosina sat quietly, petting Hercules.

"You've recently been tangled up with those gang raids the police were doing across Toronto, right?"

"Yes, the Angels of Violence are done."

"And the Leap Year Killer was taken care of."

"You read a lot of papers."

"I need to." He paused to sip his grappa. "Gives me peace of mind."

"And me," Rosina chimed in.

"What's your story?" Sarah asked again. "I'm sorry if that's an intrusive question, but you've really intrigued me. I saw the scars on your arms. I'm curious; what have you two been through?"

Darwin coughed into his hand and cleared his throat. He took another drink and then got up to refill his glass.

"When I lived in Toronto many years ago, I wrote thrillers for a living. Then my wife and I found ourselves in a real-life thriller. I've written all about it in a novel called *Sharp Fear*."

"What a coincidence. I've been writing my memoirs. I've completed two manuscripts already, and when I return to Toronto, I will start on my third."

"Wow, that's fantastic. Tell us a bit about it."

Sarah spent the next half an hour regaling them with tales of crimes, kidnappings, and sadistic killers and how her sister helped her stop them.

When she was done, Darwin started in on his tale of getting caught up with the mafia and how it turned their lives upside down for quite a while. He seemed guarded, and she suspected he only gave part of the real story. He talked about how he got the nickname, The Blade, even though he couldn't stand the sight of knives, and how eventually he had to go after the people terrorizing him and his wife to end the nightmare.

But since they'd been in Italy, everything had stopped. If anyone were still looking for them, they would have no idea where to start. Italy, the home of the mafia, would be the last place they would look.

The three of them sat stunned at how their lives had brought them together. The bottle of grappa was empty, and Sarah felt comfortably numb.

"You took a risk telling me all that," Sarah said. "Why?"

They looked at each other and then back to Sarah. "We've followed what you've done in the past and just recently with those gangs. After meeting you … well, let's just say we know you're safe. Were we wrong to assume this?"

"No, absolutely not." Sarah shook her head, hair brushing her cheeks.

For the first time in a long time, she felt safe.

The baby monitor registered a sniffle. Then a cry.

"I got it." Rosina got up.

After she was gone, Darwin turned to Sarah. "You're here after Sam Marconi, aren't you?"

"How did you know?"

"I read Italian newspapers, too. He's spent the last year or more terrorizing the mafia, the very people he used to work for."

"What can you tell me about him?"

"Come on into my office."

Sarah followed him through the living room, the kitchen, and then down a hallway.

"Wait, can I get some water?" she asked.

"Sure. Make yourself at home." Darwin turned around in the hall and pointed. "My office is the last door."

Sarah entered the kitchen, found the glasses, poured water, and drank it all down. The grappa had gone to her head, even on a full stomach. Outside the kitchen window, the dark night pushed against the pane. Her face reflected in the window, casting a hollow look back, bags under her sad eyes.

Aaron ...

She drank once more, set the glass on the counter, and walked the hall to Darwin's office.

Inside, the walls were plastered with faces. Pictures of men and some women lined the walls in pyramid formations with tiny white cards under their photos, names written in red ink. Each pyramid was inside what looked like the drawing of a country in the background.

"What's all this?"

"I monitor the major mafia families throughout the world. I try to track where they are and what they're doing in each country. Mostly I'm doing something akin to CIA."

"Akin to CIA?"

"I listen to chatter over the internet."

"Chatter? What are you listening for?"

"My name or Rosina's."

"Wow, you're serious about security."

"After what happened to us and the people I had to deal with, I have to be."

Hercules entered the office.

"Hercules, nein." He moved toward the door and pointed down the hallway. "Gehen. Jetzt."

Hercules lowered his head, turned, and left the office.

"What was that? It sounded like German."

"It was. I told him no. Then I told him to go now. He's not allowed in the office."

"He knows German?"

"I have enemies in Canada, the States, and Italy. I don't have any enemies in Germany that I'm aware of. If any of them find us and Hercules is the first to discover them, I want no confusion about what commands he will respond to. If I yell the word 'no' and I'm referring to Rosina or Bradley, but Hercules hesitates, it could all end right there. Besides, he is a *German* shepherd."

Rosina entered the office through the open door. "Herc trying to get in here again?"

Darwin nodded as he searched a file folder in a cabinet by his large desk.

"Ahh, here it is." He pulled out a file and browsed the pages. "Marconi got his name from dealing card games over fifteen years ago. Underground casinos in the backs of barber shops, you know the kind. He would deal games for the big boys, have them served alcohol, and eventually, because he was so good with the cards, would deal whoever he was working for that night the right hands."

"So he started as a crook."

"Which one of these guys didn't?"

She nodded.

Darwin scanned a page with his finger. "Eventually, someone caught on. A fight broke out. The Dealer executed the guy and protected his employer, who later became a powerful man. The Dealer went on to bigger and better things." Darwin looked up. "That's about all I have on his history. More recently, I've followed his exploits, but I can tell you that without documents."

Sarah sat in a chair in the corner of the office, and Rosina took the other one. "What's he been up to? Why did the Italian authorities call the FBI for help?"

Darwin sat down at his desk. "Funny you should ask because I don't think they did."

She thought about the fraud Kierian had become.

Darwin said, "I think the Italian authorities called the FDA for help."

"The Food and Drug Administration?" Sarah asked, taken aback. "Why would they do that?"

"They also called Interpol."

"I'm confused."

"Smoke and mirrors."

She turned to Rosina. "Does he always talk like this?" She looked back at Darwin. "I'm full, I'm probably drunk, and I'm tired. Can you spell it out easier for me?"

"Of course. Marconi has killed a couple of his rivals in La Cosa Nostra as smoke and mirrors and to enable his drug trade and prostitution rings. Still, it was only to cover up the one important murder he claims responsibility for."

"Which is?"

"The murder of the agricultural minister here in Italy. I gained access to his personal emails. Since then, I've been trying to hack into the finance minister's emails and the minister of the environment."

Thoroughly confused, Sarah asked, "Why hack into their

emails?"

"So I can check itineraries, see where they're going, who they're talking to. But it's one of the hardest things for me to do. Maybe tomorrow, the day after, next week, or next month, I'll get into their emails. Who knows?"

"Back up a second. Why would Marconi kill an agricultural guy?"

"Because of the conference being held here in Umbertide next week. Three ministers have written a decree that will go live in six days to ban the use of GMOs in Italy. Those three ministers are the agricultural minister, deceased, the minister of the environment, and the health minister. The latter two are in hiding until the conference."

"Why does the minister of finance interest you, then?"

"Because he's one of the loudest voices against this decree, and he's a crook. I think he gets kickbacks from the company that wants to bring GMOs into Italy."

"I've heard of GMOs, but can you elaborate in simple terms, considering the hour?"

"Genetically modified organism. Basically, it's the process of taking the genes of one organism and forcing it into the DNA of another, hence genetically modifying it."

"Why would anyone do that?" Sarah asked.

"I asked the same question and did my research. For example, they have added fish DNA to the DNA of tomatoes."

"Eww, why?"

"If you have a tomato crop and the temperatures were to drop below zero unseasonably, they would freeze and be no good to anyone. Scientists decided to look at what allowed the DNA of the arctic flounder, a fish that can survive in extremely cold temperatures, to withstand the cold. They then took the DNA of the fish and inserted it in the tomato seed. Now when the tomato freezes, it can withstand the cold, and the farmer doesn't lose the crop."

"That sounds fantastic, but who would want to eat tomatoes with fish DNA in them?"

"Exactly. And it goes deeper."

"You have a lot of time on your hands."

"You have no idea." Darwin winked at Rosina and then looked back at Sarah. "They inserted spider genes into goat's DNA to extract the protein found in the spider web out of the goat's milk."

"You're kidding, right?" Sarah stared at Darwin, who didn't flinch. She looked at Rosina for support.

"He's not kidding," Rosina said.

A realization hit Sarah. "Is that why our kidnapper told me to watch what I eat?"

"Kidnapper?"

"Yeah, that staged attack at Aaron's apartment I told you about. Where I was warned to stay out of Italy. He told me to watch what I eat."

Darwin and Rosina exchanged a glance.

"I think the other two ministers are in danger. It has scared us to have so many powerful people in Umbertide since we live so close. But we'll stay near the house for those few days until everyone leaves. We'll be in lockdown."

"I'm going to have to talk to my colleague in the States to find out what the authorities are up to regarding my absence from the hotel room in Rome. After that, I want to visit this conference and see if I can find Marconi."

"You may be able to meet him earlier than that. He's

going to be in Umbertide for a few days before the conference."

"How would you know that?"

"If you were Marconi, wouldn't you scope the place out?"

She agreed with a nod.

"Also," Darwin said, getting up from his chair. "That investigative reporter will probably be here."

She remembered Kierian talking about an investigative reporter.

"I was supposed to meet a reporter in Rome."

"That would make sense. This guy has been all over the GMO use in corn and soy and what it's doing to crops worldwide. He's the loudest voice in Italy against GMOs, but he's had to go underground because of death threats. His online name is an alias. No one knows his real name or what he looks like. Some claim he's a myth, but I think he's real."

"What's his online name?"

"The Cowboy."

Shocked, Sarah sat up straighter. "You're kidding?"

"Why that response?"

"A man was following me in Rome wearing a cowboy hat and boots."

"You can't be sure it's the same man, but if he was following you, and you and the FBI man were supposed to meet him, then it might be." Darwin walked to a cabinet on the side wall. He opened a drawer and pulled out a box.

"I've got something for you." Darwin opened the box and retrieved a small black gun. "It's a sig sauer pro, semi-automatic. Weighs about twenty-seven ounces and packs a punch. The U.S. Army uses them, as does the French police."

"This is for me?" Sarah asked.

"Do you have a gun?"

Sarah shook her head.

"Didn't think so. Here." He pushed the box into her hands. "Due to security reasons and the safety of our home and baby, you can stay the night, but I'll have to ask you to leave in the morning and not return. I don't want to sound rude, but I'm sure you understand."

"Of course."

"Take the gun when you leave, and make sure I read about your successes in the newspapers."

Sarah hugged Darwin and Rosina and told them she would retire to the guest bedroom. "I'll talk to my sister, and then I'll meet this cowboy and find out what I can. If I need to use this," she held the box in the air, "I'll make you proud."

Darwin wrapped an arm around his wife.

"If you can, make sure Marconi has an accident. That would be present enough."

She wasn't sure, but Darwin's eyes seemed to water when he said Marconi's name. She wondered what the connection was.

"Good night, then," she said.

"Buonanotte."

Sarah got to her room, undressed, and slipped into bed, the loaded weapon under her pillow.

She dreamed of Aaron lost at sea. When she woke, her pillow was soaked in sweat and tears.

Chapter 26

THE MORNING SUN BROKE through the curtains of the guest room, rousing her from sleep. A rooster crowed in the distance. The soft breeze from outside the window caressed her skin. She didn't want to get up or ever leave this house. She yearned for this kind of peace but knew it would be many years until she could stop working with Vivian and enjoy a home like this.

Sarah grabbed the paper on the table beside the bed. Nothing was written on it, even though she had moved it during the night.

I'm lost in Italy here, Vivian. Could use some help.

She collected herself, used the bathroom, dressed, and headed to the kitchen. Rosina was already up and feeding Bradley.

"Good morning," Sarah said.

"Good morning. Fresh fruit from the market is on the

table under the pergola outside. Darwin's already out there."

"Thanks." Sarah meandered around the table, a floor plant, and then through the double doors that led out to the back.

"Morning, Darwin."

"Sleep well?"

"Much needed."

"Ready for today?"

She shielded her eyes from the sun. "Something specific happening today?"

"Sam Marconi is in town."

"How would you know that? Don't tell me he publishes his travel itinerary online."

Darwin shook his head. "Nothing like that. I've got websites that enable me to monitor cell phones geographically. In the past few months, I was able to get the cell phone numbers of two of his closest associates. They're all moving toward Umbertide."

"Wow, you're quite something."

"Is that a compliment?"

"Absolutely." Sarah grabbed a small bowl on the table and filled it with chunks of kiwi, an orange, sliced pear, and apples.

"Can you be ready in half an hour?" Darwin asked.

"Of course. What's on the agenda?"

"I'll drive you close to town and drop you off. We're locking the place up tight Jand staying inside. Only Hercules will remain on the outside. I'll watch the house with cameras at least until these guys depart. Until then, we're in full lockdown here."

"I'm so sorry you two have to live this way."

"We're happy. We have each other and Bradley. Most of the time, we're regular folks, buying groceries, watching movies, and reading, always reading. Only when I detect powerful underworld criminals getting close to our city do we take certain precautions."

"Makes sense. I'll be ready."

Rosina joined them, and they ate breakfast together. Half an hour later, Sarah got in the passenger seat of the Fiat, and Darwin drove her into town.

"You have the Sig Sauer?"

"Right here," Sarah patted her waist. "I wanted to thank you and your wife for such warm hospitality. You two are a class act."

"Sarah, we're out of the fight. We watch and listen, but it doesn't look like anyone even remembers us anymore. You're still in the fight. You are the hero here. Keep it up and stay alive. We'd be pretty sad if anything happened to you."

She teared up. It had been many years since she had met such heart-on-their-sleeve kind of people.

"Just remember," Darwin added. "For the safety of my family, you can't come back to the house."

She nodded, completely understanding. "No offense taken," she said with a smile. "I wouldn't be able to find it, anyway."

"Maybe one day, when Bradley is a teenager, we won't have to live like this. On that day, we'll have you and Aaron over. Deal?"

"It's a deal. I'll look forward to it. I'll be in my mid-thirties and ready to settle down by then."

"I should hope so."

They remained silent for the rest of the ride. Darwin

pulled up short of the Tiber River and parked in an empty restaurant parking lot.

"Walk across that bridge and stay on this road. It'll take you into the heart of Umbertide."

"Where can I get an espresso?"

"The best one in town is called Antico Caffè Giardino. He's right on this road. Just cross the bridge and stay to the right."

They hugged over the stick shift.

"Goodbye, Darwin."

"Goodbye, Sarah. Stay alive."

As she got out, she said, "Say goodbye to your lovely wife for me."

"I will," Darwin shouted back as he pulled away.

Moments later, Sarah was alone in the parking lot of a restaurant with a gun stuck in her pants by her belly button.

The relaxation of Darwin's home had sapped her motivation to figure everything out.

She turned and walked toward town, determined to get her head back in the game.

At Antico Caffè, she ordered an espresso and drank it at the counter like Italians did. She also ordered a cornetto, a small croissant with apple filling.

Then she asked the man with the curly black hair behind the counter where she could find an internet spot.

He directed her one block down the street.

When she got to Infomatica, a man set her in a corner booth right up against the window that looked out onto the street.

As she sat down, a man entered the internet store. She reached for her gun and almost pulled it out to shoot him. It was the same man with the ponytail who had smiled at her on the train from Rome. No one followed her without consequences. He stood at the counter.

Was it a coincidence he was here? Or *was* he following her?

Before she left the internet shop, she would find out what he was up to and who he was, or she'd send him on a guided tour of the local hospital.

Chapter 27

Frank had spent the entire day walking the streets of
Umbertide, looking for any sign of Sarah or the cowboy. He
should've killed the cowboy when he had the chance, but
Sarah was the target.

And now she was gone.

He was so sure that Sarah would be in Umbertide that he
did not leave the city. Marconi would be here today to attend
the dinner meeting that night, leaving Frank with no choice
but to wait it out.

What other city would Sarah go to? He walked through
the main piazza in the center of Umbertide as the noon sun
warmed the cobblestones under his feet. He tried to see the
benefit of Sarah on the run somewhere else in Italy but
couldn't. If the only place she ever spent any time in were
Umbertide and Montone, she would come here. Montone was
small and off the train line. From what he read, there had

been a massive shootout with some kind of militia group, and Sarah had been involved briefly before she went back to Hungary a few years ago.

Frank passed the city's circular church as he worked himself into a frenzy in an attempt to create an alternative for Sarah, but no matter how many times he broke it down, Umbertide had to be her destination.

Yet she didn't show up on that train. Nor had he seen her in any of the more popular tourist spots.

Before siesta came and the shops closed until later in the afternoon, he needed to call in, but he had destroyed his phone and scattered the pieces across the tracks at the train station.

Infomatica, the only internet store in Umbertide, came up on his right.

He would call his boss, who he hadn't spoken to since yesterday, and tell him everything was on track.

As Infomatica came into view, so did a woman with blonde hair flowing over her shoulder. The woman had a familiar walk. She stopped in front of Infomatica for a moment, then stepped inside.

What luck.

It was destiny or fate that he decided to go to Infomatica at the same time as Sarah Roberts. He would be nonchalant. He would pretend not to notice her. He would be smooth.

It made him irresistible. Sarah was a woman and, like any woman, could be seduced. Like the immune system discovering the code of a persistent virus, he would determine her defenses and break them down. She would melt in his hands like a box of Smarties squished in his palm on a hot day. It would only be a matter of time. Some girls took longer than others, though.

Sarah wouldn't be too hard.

He smiled to himself as he approached the doors of the internet shop.

Won't she be surprised, he thought.

Maybe he could bed her down before he put a bullet through her forehead.

Chapter 28

S ARAH KEPT HER HEAD down and waited to see what the man would do. He approached the counter and talked in rapid Italian to the clerk. After a moment the clerk produced a piece of paper and pointed to the open cubicle beside her.

Perfect.

During the exchange, the man from the train didn't look at Sarah once. She opened the icon on her computer, brought up Skype, and signed in. She put the headphones on and started the process of calling Parkman.

From the corner of her eye, she watched as the man walked over, sat beside her, and turned his system on. He also opened Skype and slipped on headphones.

Maybe it was just a coincidence. Just because they were on the same train two days ago could mean nothing. Dozens of people took the same train. By any other rationale, having met Darwin and Rosina, or even Jonas Saul, held a diabolical meaning of some kind. She had to be careful not to see the darker side of people first. That was a lesson the generous Darwin and Rosina had taught her in the last twenty-four hours.

Parkman picked up at his end, but instead of talking where anyone who understood English could overhear her, Sarah typed.

Is there anything new on Aaron?

Nothing, Parkman typed. *Can't get anyone to tell me anything. But I am hearing a lot about you.*

Me? Like what?

Almost every police officer and their neighbor are looking for you. They're assuming you've fled the country by now. Stay low wherever you are and stay off the streets.

Can't do that. She leaned back in her chair to stretch her arms to see if the ponytail man was watching her. Then she sat forward again. *I have to figure this shit out. It'll all come together this week.*

Just be careful. A dead Sarah doesn't help anyone.

Parkman, can you look into an investigative reporter working in Italy called The Cowboy?

Of course. When do you want this?

I'll try to contact you at the same time tomorrow.

In the middle of the night? It may be almost one in the afternoon where you are, but it's four in the morning here.

Sorry, I'll wait until the evening. Tomorrow night then?

A car pulled up out front. It stopped too fast. Four men jumped out. The clerk didn't pay any attention. Ponytail man beside her had his head down as he studied his screen.

The four men acted wrong to her. They examined the street with their backs to the internet spot, watching for something.

Parkman, gotta run. Chat soon. Sarah signed off and erased her history.

At the window, one of the men lifted his hands to the sides of his face and pressed up against the glass to look in. When he did, his jacket opened enough to expose the gun resting on his ribcage.

Shit!

Sarah ripped the headphones off her head and rose from her chair.

***

Frank was reeling at the luck of not only finding her but being able to sit beside her. When he entered the internet spot, he spoke Italian to the clerk, using rare Italian words to tell him that he needed this specific booth. The clerk didn't even bat an eye.

As Frank sat, he caught the briefest glance of Skype on Sarah's computer. It was perfect. He needed to call in, too.

After logging in, he dialed his employer. Once on the phone, he typed.

I've got the subject. I'm ready to move forward.

His employer typed back. *You're too late.*

How's that? Our arrangement allows until tonight.

You went offline. It worried me. You went rogue. The gambler is no longer your target. Nor is the subject you refer to. I'm sticking to the original plan.

The original plan?

The gambler went rogue, doing his own thing. That was the reason for hiring you. But he's back and assured me he's on the same agenda.

You're not in a position to cancel my contract. It is non-negotiable.

Consider it canceled. This is our last communication. I will not take calls from you, nor am I associated with you.

The screen changed as his employer clicked off.

Frank hadn't expected that. He should have seen it coming. Since Sarah had been his main focus, he must have lost touch with the reality of the job. There would be consequences. His employer had to be held accountable.

He had never been fired before. He never wanted to be fired again. It angered him in ways he couldn't imagine and led him to the only logical conclusion.

His employer couldn't be allowed to live. The cost involved with having someone out there who felt he had failed in his task would have the potential to hurt his twelve-year reputation. He hadn't failed, though. Nothing had changed. The employer got cold feet, that was all. Cold feet killed men. Cold feet were a weakness, and lack of strength was what Charles Darwin spoke of when he said the survival of the fittest.

Frank was mentally and physically fit. The job would continue as planned, but now there was an addendum. His employer just got added to the list of executions.

It began on Frank's terms, and it ended on Frank's terms. That's the way it had always been and would always be.

Sarah's head rose beside him. He clicked out of Skype, erased his history on the browser, and closed it down.

It was time to talk to Sarah. Time to get her to trust him. Then he would invite her to dinner and enjoy her company, possibly her young body.

When he turned toward her, she stood up so fast her headphones ripped from her head, and the chair smacked against the wall.

She had a small black gun in her hand.

What the fuck?

Then the front panes of the internet spot shattered into a million pieces, covering them in the glass.

***

The man outside Infomatica peered through the glass at Sarah as she got up and then at the man with the ponytail beside her. Like a dark curtain, recognition draped across his face. He either knew her or the man with the ponytail.

Or both of us.

She barely caught his Italian commands through the glass, but the rest of the men heard him perfectly.

They drew their weapons in unison and turned to the windows.

Sarah yanked out her Sig. The man with the ponytail turned to look at her.

Then the windows shattered, showering her in tiny shards of glass.

She ducked and covered her head, shouting as the weapons outside the store burst out a scary staccato. She raised the Sig to shoot blind, but there was no recoil. It didn't fire.

The safety.

She dove for the tile floor behind Ponytail's chair and landed hard, already rolling behind the large counter where the smart clerk had dropped.

More gunfire shattered the afternoon calm. Lights in the ceiling shattered, roof tiles shredded, and the glass display cabinet behind the counter showered them with more tiny pieces of glass.

"Fuck!" Sarah shouted.

The ponytail man landed hard by the edge of the counter. Sarah raised her weapon, flicked off the safety, and almost put a round through his face. He dragged himself to safety behind the counter using his arms.

"Bloody hell!" he shouted. "Don't shoot me." He studied the gun in her hand as bits of glass fell on his stomach. "Do you know how to use that thing?"

She nodded.

"Then help." He got up on one knee and raised his gun over the counter, firing indiscriminately.

Sarah did the same. She fired at the now retreating men. Two were sprawled on the floor, bleeding from wounds created by Ponytail.

Good shot.

The other two headed for the parked car. She saved her bullets as the men weren't a threat anymore.

Ponytail took careful aim. As the man getting into the passenger seat was about to shut the door, Ponytail fired again.

The man's head rocked back, one of his eyes disappearing in a dark orb of blood. He dropped forward, slumped against the dash, and stopped moving. The driver turned the car on, shoved his dead passenger out the door, and hit the gas. The car door slammed shut with the forward motion.

"What the hell was that?" Sarah asked as she got to her

feet. "Were they after you or someone else?" She kept her weapon in her hand, safety off in case Ponytail was a problem.

He slipped his weapon away and stood up.

"We need to leave."

"I'm not going anywhere with you," Sarah shouted. She looked him up and down. "Who the fuck *are* you?"

"I'm the cowboy you were supposed to meet in Rome. I'm the investigative reporter, and those men were trying to silence me. They don't want me talking to you."

Chapter 29

A PEDESTRIAN TUNNEL LED under the tracks two blocks away at the train station.

Inside the tunnel, Sarah stood on one side, her back pressed against the graffiti-laden wall, the Sig firmly in her hand. The Cowboy tried to explain his presence at the internet spot from the other wall.

"I watched you and the FBI man from the moment you got to Termini," Cowboy said. "I was supposed to make contact, but I was waiting until I was absolutely sure the coast was clear. When I saw that other man dressed as a cowboy, I knew I had to be careful."

"Who is the other man dressed as a cowboy?" Sarah asked.

He shrugged. "I have no idea, but I think he killed your FBI friend."

"First, he wasn't FBI, nor was he my friend. Second, I

can't tell if you're lying. Until I'm sure I want your gun."

The man extended his arms away from his sides in an exaggerated gesture of compliance. "I have it for protection. The articles I've written about GMOs have garnered death threats." He eased the gun out. "I want this back as soon as you can learn to trust me."

She gestured for him to drop it with the tip of her Sauer.

"I'll kick it over. But you'll take care of it, right?"

She nodded.

"When will I get it back?"

She raised the Sig and stepped closer. "Drop it and kick it over, or you'll never need to worry about it again."

"Please, you have to trust me." He set the gun on the concrete and kicked it hard enough to bump the wall beside Sarah.

She lowered her gun but didn't put it away. "Do you have any other weapons on you?"

He shook his head.

"Are you aware of the penalty for lying to me?"

He looked confused.

"Then I'll tell you." She pointed at his crotch. "An entire magazine emptied in there to make you a woman. Would you like that?"

"Why are you so mean? I'm on your side."

"First, I'm not being mean. I do what I do to stay alive. Second, I'll determine if you're on my side."

"You don't call what you said mean?"

"You're still alive. I'm being nice." She knelt to pick up his weapon. "I trust no one. I was told that my colleague and I were supposed to meet an investigative reporter. Since then, I can't trust anyone, which includes you. Convince me otherwise. Why shouldn't I kill you right now? Give me something juicy to spare your life because I'm sick and tired of people lying to me."

The Cowboy looked both ways and cleared his throat. He wiped his face with his hand. "I'll tell you what I know." He paused as a train rumbled overhead. "Your name is Sarah Roberts. You're in Italy to meet with me. I was expecting to meet with the FBI as well, but you're saying he wasn't FBI."

She nodded and rolled her hand in a circle a few times. "Anybody could read an online newspaper and know who I am. Talk faster. I want meat with my dinner."

"I've written many articles against GMOs and been fired from my job a couple of times. I want Italy to remain the strong agricultural country we're known for, not the puppet of some biotech company with its team of white-coated scientists. There's a man named Sam Marconi that has been known to run in mafia circles. Every reporter knows his name. I believe he murdered the agricultural minister, and I believe he wants to kill two more ministers before he's done."

"How would you know this?"

"I'm an investigative reporter. It's what I do. There's a conference coming up in Umbertide at the end of the week. These three ministers have signed a decree to ban GMOs. Once it comes out at the conference, it'll be published and become legal. But if they're dead during or before the conference, not much will happen with the decree. I think someone high up is orchestrating everything."

"Pull out your cell phone."

"I don't have one on me."

She narrowed her eyes. "Don't lie. I've warned you

about lying."

"Seriously, I don't."

"How do you stay in contact with anyone? How could you call for help?"

"Yell?"

"You're not a comedian. Something isn't right about this. You're hiding something."

"I swear, I'm not."

The Cowboy had broken out in a sweat.

"Wedding ring?" Sarah asked. "You married?"

He shook his head.

"Let me see your hands."

He held them up. On the index finger of his right hand sat a gold ring. She moved closer and took the finger in her hand.

"What's this ring?" she asked, studying it.

"I got it from my mother when I first took the job at the ___"

Sarah flipped his hand around and twisted his wrist back. Then she pulled his wrist at a ninety-degree angle into her body and bore weight down on it until he screamed and dropped to one knee in front of her.

"What the fuck?" he yelled at her, his voice cracking.

Sarah bent close to his ear. "Tell me the truth. You're lying to me about something."

"No. I'm not. You have to believe me."

"I don't. You fired that weapon too good to be a reporter."

"Father was in the military. Taught me at ranges." He moaned and tried to get closer to the ground. "Ahhh, you're going to break my wrist."

She slapped his back pockets and felt along his belt line. Upon quick inspection, she found no other weapon or cell phone.

She released his wrist and stood back, the Sig still ready.

He rolled on his side and caressed his wounded wrist. "I came to help you," he said. "And this is how I get treated?"

"Who were those men after? You or me or both of us?"

"Me. I'm sure of it."

"Why?"

"Because Marconi is in town tonight. He wants me dead, as does his employer."

"Who's his employer?"

Cowboy started to get up. "You know, I don't think I want to talk to you anymore."

She stepped inside his space again and placed the weapon on his crotch. "You don't get options. We do it my way, or I'll save Marconi the trouble."

"Okay, okay."

"I'm the closest thing to a friend you've got."

"That so?" he asked. "I'd hate to see my enemy."

"You're not funny. Stop trying to be."

"Neither are you."

"The difference is I'm not trying to be. Now move."

"Where are we going?"

"We'll continue this in a quiet corner of a café somewhere. If those men come back and find us down here, we'll have bought a one-way pass out of this train station to shit knows where."

He nodded and started walking, still massaging his wrist.

"You walk ahead. Funny stuff gets you a bullet in the ass. You'll remember how funny you were every time you had to sit on the toilet. Stupid stuff gets a bullet in the crotch. I don't have to tell you how bad it'll be when you're about to have sex, and remember that you're dickless." She pushed his shoulder. "Walk faster."

***

As Frank brilliantly spewed details to Sarah, an idea formed. He could finger his employer, and when Sarah made contact with whoever she was working with, an investigation would start. Maybe the best revenge wasn't killing his weak-ass employer. Maybe the best revenge was watching as he was indicted on conspiracy to commit murder charges.

But Sarah had ruined the idea of seducing her. As soon as she let her guard down, he would kill her. There would be no waiting until the dinner meeting tonight. No waiting on anything. She had nearly broken his wrist, and she would pay dearly for that.

He walked ahead, sizing up each turn they made, each block they walked, waiting to surprise her.

He was done playing by the rules. She should have been executed in Rome. It wasn't his fault that she wasn't in the room when he got there and saw that FBI man dead.

What the hell was going on anyway? Why did he come all the way to Italy only to kill himself on the balcony of his own hotel room? And now Sarah said he wasn't even FBI.

Who the hell is Sarah working for? If Marconi was hired to kill the ministers and added two mafia dons to the list on his own, and Frank was hired to finish the job, Marconi started by killing Marconi first, then who hired Sarah?

Now that Marconi was hunting him and almost got him

at the internet spot, he had to watch his back diligently. Walking out in the open like this was risky. They had to get inside somewhere.

He looked back. Sarah was far enough away that he couldn't grab her but close enough to pull her weapon and shoot him if he tried to run.

But he wouldn't run. He had her right where he wanted her. They were together, and he would use whatever charm he still possessed to woo her into trusting him.

But any time he got the chance, he would take her out.

He would stomp on her head with his boots for hurting his wrist the way she did. For humiliating him and hurting his pride, he would stomp on her chest.

For threatening his manhood, he would stomp on her crotch until that hole was double the size. Then he would fuck her with a grenade and pull the pin when he was done.

The image of Sarah exploding from within made him smile.

Man, am I going to love killing this stupid bitch.

Chapter 30

THEY FOUND A LARGE café that was nearly empty as the siesta had started. Most businesses closed from one-thirty p.m. until around three-thirty p.m. to avoid the hottest part of the day. It had become such a custom that the Italians did it even in the colder months.

After ordering two cappuccinos, they sat in the far corner. Sarah placed the Sig on her lap.

"My piece is aimed at you. The safety is off. We're going to talk. If you so much as twitch, I'll twitch, too. You don't want me to twitch."

He nodded as he raised his coffee cup slowly.

"Now, talk," she said. "Where's Marconi going to be?"

"In the square called April 25, at a restaurant."

"Why did they name the square a date?"

"At the end of World War II, April 25 was the date Italy was liberated from the Nazis."

"Oh." Sarah nodded. "It's a good name, then. Tell me about the restaurant."

"It's called Capitone."

"How do you know about this?"

"I won't reveal my sources. You can shoot me, but I'll never reveal my sources. Even in a court of law, my sources stay with me."

"Honorable. Admirable. But I don't care. How do you know about this dinner?"

He looked down at his cup and stirred the milk froth on top.

Sarah kicked him under the table. "What do you think this is? A fucking game? I ask a question, I get an answer." She kicked him again. "If you're some asshole who's here to kill me or Marconi or the ministers at the conference or all of us, then your stupidity will give you away. But if you're really The Cowboy, then we're on the same side, and I need to know everything. It's a matter of my life and your death."

He looked up and met her gaze. "I often use illegal means to get the information I need."

"Now we're getting somewhere."

"I'm not proud of what I do," Frank said.

Kick me again, Frank thought. *I'll shove that foot so far up your pretty little ass it'll come out your mouth.*

"What did you do to learn about Marconi in Umbertide?"

He was beginning to think she would never believe him. Was there anything he could say that would get her to believe him? He wracked his brain, trying to remember anything he could about that fucking Cowboy, but he couldn't. He would just have to wing it and hope she took the bait.

Otherwise, he would kill the stupid whore in a café in

Umbertide for the world to see.

His breaking point was near, the edge close. One more disrespectful act from Sarah, just one, and he would teach her some manners.

I hope she believes me, or she'll end up dead over her cappuccino.

Frank opened his mouth and continued to lie.

"I tracked Marconi's cell phone. Then I used illegal software to hack into his phone. I was able to hear everything."

Was he lying? Sarah couldn't tell. Is there software that allows people to do this? Are the days of planting bugs over?

"Why not take this to the authorities?" she said. "Let them track Marconi and arrest him."

"The information was obtained illegally. It would never hold up in court."

She nodded. "Why aren't you wearing a cowboy hat if you're The Cowboy?"

"Are you kidding?"

"Look at my face." She gave him a blank stare. "Do you think I'm kidding?"

He shook his head.

"You'll know when I'm kidding," she added. "I'll have wine in one hand, a smile on my face, music playing, and people dancing. I'll crack a sour joke, and we'll pretend to laugh. That's me, kidding. This isn't. Catch the difference?"

His eye twitched briefly.

"What's wrong?" she asked. "Muscle spasm? Or anger?"

"Fear," he mumbled. "You scare me."

"Good." She didn't believe him. "Now answer the fucking question."

"I got the nickname The Cowboy because of my reckless nature in the articles I write." He paused to clear his throat. "I write about hot subjects and call people to answer for their actions. I didn't get the name because of how I dress, and I didn't change how I dress because of the name."

"What can you tell me about the conference coming to Umbertide?"

"The man who hired Marconi will be there. I know that."

"Who is he?"

The ponytail man almost looked happy to say his name.

"The Minister of Finance, Silvio Capelli."

"And this Capelli wants to have the other two ministers killed? Is that what you're telling me?"

The ponytail man nodded.

"Bit harsh, isn't it? Aren't there other ways to veto a bill? Vote it down, hold meetings, and lobby for change. Isn't that what politicians do?"

"I can't speak for Capelli's motivations. Each man knows intimately what drives him."

"What drives you?"

"Truth."

"What's your real name? I won't call you The Cowboy."

"I don't reveal—"

She kicked him hard under the table.

His hands rose, and for a brief second, his face changed, then settled back. He set his hands on the tabletop.

"I'd appreciate it if you stopped doing that."

"Fuck you." She brought the gun above the table. The café was empty, and the woman behind the counter had gone to the back. "Someone showed up at my hotel in Rome and shot the man I came to Italy with. Government officials are hiring mafia hitmen. You're following me. I see a cowboy in Rome, but you're claiming to be him." She sipped the end of her cappuccino. "And you want to be evasive? Well, fuck you. I get the answers I want, or I send you to the hospital. You'll get out in a few weeks. By then, all this will be over, and I'll be back home, a glass of wine in my hand. Get it? Answers or hospital. At least I'm giving you options. Can't say that about those four thugs who tried to kill us an hour ago."

***

"My name is Frank De Luca."

He decided to give her his real name because no one knew it. The more he lied, the more he would have to lie to keep covering it up.

That last kick almost made him dive across the table and wrap his hands around her throat.

He couldn't play around anymore. It was time to lay it out and then catch her off guard. She would have to use the bathroom soon. She would walk back into town with him. She would do something that would unwittingly give him the upper hand, and then he would strike, and when he did, she would feel it.

The hospital?

It'll be a morgue for you, bitch.

Sometime within the next hour or so, he would kill her. He'd jab the cappuccino spoon in her eye if he had to.

I'm going to enjoy that moment.

***

Sarah saw something in his eyes change. A determination. Something that made her yearn for contact from Vivian.

Where have you been, Vivian?

She wouldn't shoot him in the café unless he made her. But she was pretty sure he wasn't The Cowboy at this point. But who was he then? Kierian's executioner? And why did those men show up at the internet spot and shoot at him? Why put Ponytail man in danger if she was their intended target?

He shot and killed three of the four men at Infomatica. She could safely say they weren't working together. So who was he, and who did he work for?

Was Marconi really going to be in Umbertide at a restaurant called Capitone in five or six hours?

There were too many questions, and no one she trusted to give her the right answers.

Except Vivian.

It was time to get paper and pen and be alone for a while. Either Vivian offered some divine wisdom, or Sarah would be completely lost.

"Get up," she ordered.

"Why? Where are we going?"

"You're getting on the next train out of Umbertide."

"What? Why? Where am I going?"

"I said get up."

He got to his feet slowly. "But I came to help you with this case. Why would you send me away?"

"Stop with the act, or I'll shoot you for persisting in the lie you're living."

"But I'm not lying—"

She rushed him, grabbed his throat with her free hand, and brought the gun up to his temple. His back smacked into the café's window.

"You're lying to me. Stop talking, or I'll stop you. My tolerance level is very low today. I might have laughed at your stupid attempt to act like a journalist any other day, but today is not that day."

His eyes took on an evil she had only seen in murderers like Armond Stuart and Death, the leader of a violent street gang. It was like his eyes took on a redness all of their own.

She almost shot him in the head to make the world a better place.

"You'll get on that train and leave town," she said. "How it works is, if I see you again, I kill you. That's it. Plain and simple. I don't bluff."

He nodded ever so slightly.

She pulled the gun away, let go of his throat, and stepped back.

"Now move."

She followed him out and down to the train station, the gun tucked away, hidden, her hand remaining firm on the butt of the weapon.

At the train station, she bought a ticket for Sansepolcro. The train was coming in five minutes.

"Any last words?" she asked.

He shook his head.

"Too afraid to say anything?"

"Just saddened that you don't believe me. I'm here to help."

"I'm not the psychic one; my sister is. But I predict

you'll return even though I'm warning you against it. I predict that I'll kill you, and you won't like that very much."

He looked down the track, avoiding her eyes.

"If you're really The Cowboy, you won't come back because you're not welcome here. I know what I need to know to end this, and I couldn't live with myself if the innocent journalist got hurt. But if you're not The Cowboy, you'll return because someone hired you to do a job, and that job isn't done."

He looked back at her, squinting in the sun.

"Therefore," she continued, "if you return to Umbertide, you're my enemy." She leaned in close, tightened her jaw, and clenched her teeth. "I hate my enemies," she said. "Settle your affairs before you come back because you won't make it in this city an hour if you do. Clear?"

The train came around the corner. He got up slowly, took the proffered ticket, and walked to where the train would stop.

Without saying a word, he got on and took a seat. The doors closed, and the train left the station heading north.

Sarah ran from the station. She had plans for tonight's dinner with Marconi.

She also had to get a cell phone. She needed the internet to read one of The Cowboy's articles and maybe find a picture of him.

But most of all, she needed a hotel room where she could rest and wait for Vivian.

Everything counted on whether or not Vivian got in touch with her.

Everything.

Chapter 31

FRANK WAITED UNTIL THE train stopped in Città di Castello before he got off. He found a pay phone and called his driver. A half-hour later, his car showed up. Inside he had a new cell phone and a choice of five different handguns.

Killing Sarah was going to be an immense pleasure. There was nothing left to do but finish the job he was hired for.

He ordered his driver to turn around and head back to Umbertide. He was a good driver who didn't ask questions. He didn't care that Frank was in Città di Castello. All he cared about was the phone attached to his hip, and when it rang, he drove to get Frank, and he made a shitload of money being wherever Frank wanted him to be.

He would wait for Sarah to show up at the restaurant Capitone to kill her and Marconi, but he couldn't be sure she would show.

He loaded three handguns, holstered two of them, stuck the third in his pants, and watched the countryside as it passed his windows.

Won't Sarah be surprised when his face is the last thing she sees?

Twenty minutes, Sarah. Twenty minutes and I'll be back in Umbertide. Let's see how tough you are with a dozen bullets in you.

Chapter 32

SARAH COULDN'T BUY A cell phone, which was infuriating. It was explained to her in broken English that in order to buy a cell phone, she had to have either an Italian tax number, which residents had, or a passport with a local address where she was staying.

Since the internet store was closed for the investigation and repairs, she had no way of getting in touch with Parkman or finding out what was happening with Aaron.

She didn't want to be called every time a hitman was hired to kill someone somewhere in the world. What happened in foreign countries was beyond her scope. When she returned home, she would have to make a new rule to only work with Vivian in North America. No more cops or law officials. Otherwise, she would be traveling the world and never having any sort of life. If she allowed it, she would be kidnapped by the job and completely taken over.

She walked the length of the main piazza, watching the restaurant where Marconi was supposed to be in a few hours.

Instead of dwelling on what had happened up until now, she had to stay proactive. She needed to identify Marconi, see him with her own eyes, and maybe have a sit down with him. The man claiming to be The Cowboy would return. He said his name was Frank, but it didn't matter. She didn't shoot people because she felt like it. When he returned and posed a threat, he would be dealt with. In the meantime, she had two weapons, thanks to Darwin and Frank.

A change in appearance was necessary. It seemed everyone recognized her wherever she went.

At just after six in the evening, she left the small piazza where Ristorante Capitone was located and made her way out of the center of town, where she stopped at a Conad, a small grocery store. Inside, she found all the supplies she would need to disguise herself.

Now she just needed a restroom. With bag in hand, she walked to Antico Caffè and entered their restroom. She used a shaver to shave only one side of her head up around the left ear. Then she added color to her hair and applied dark eye shadow.

When she was done, she brushed her hair out and cleaned up as best as possible. Only two people knocked on the door the entire time she monopolized the bathroom.

She was now ready for the evening.

It wasn't mobsters, hitmen, or cowboys that scared her. What scared her most was not hearing from Vivian.

Why, Vivian?

The mirror reflected an image she didn't recognize. The black eye shadow rode her eyes horizontally to her temple.

The red coloring in her hair didn't come out auburn as she had hoped. It was reddish-orange, like the color of a ripe tomato.

At least I'll stand out.

Now she needed a dress. She threw everything out in Antico's restroom garbage and left, searching for a long dress for tonight's dinner.

Vivian, I could use you here. What's my play?

With Aaron in jail, no ally in Italy, her name on their hit list, whoever they were, and every authority in the country looking for her, she didn't have much hope in things working out. But walking away was never an option.

No, this job looked like it might be her last.

If they don't kill me first.

Chapter 33

Frank had his driver stop the car under a large tree in a park off one of the main roads in Umbertide. While he slept in the back seat, he instructed his driver to go for a walk and return with food by six in the evening.

At six-thirty p.m., Frank was rested, his stomach content, and he was ready. He grabbed a black jacket from the trunk and opened the spare tire compartment. A black box sat where the spare tire was supposed to be. He typed a code into the black box's keypad and opened the lid. Inside, he found what he was looking for.

He chose five small black devices with timers. They resembled squibs, small explosive devices used in military applications. These had been modified to have the power to blow a hole in a concrete wall. On the front of each unit was a small digital timer. On the back, reinforced sticky tape. A bomb squad would have a difficult time disabling any of his squibs. Ripping them off their mounts once he stuck them down was a detonator. If they were discovered and torn from their mounts, nothing would be left in a ten-foot radius of each unit.

He told his driver to meet him at ten that evening in the train station's parking lot. He placed two handguns into holsters under his jacket, took the small bombs in a backpack, and made off for Ristorante Capitone.

The only hotel inside the historical section of Umbertide was directly above the restaurant where he was headed. He used the stairs beside the restaurant and entered the hotel's main office.

"You need a room?" the old man behind a large desk asked in Italian.

"For one night," Frank said, his smile almost hitting each ear.

Once inside his room above the restaurant, he set the timers of two of the modified squibs to explode at nine that evening. Then he gently pulled the black metal protector plates off the sticky tape and set both units at stress points on the floor. When they detonated, the majority of this room would crumble into the restaurant below.

He laughed when he thought of the random customers who would die while enjoying dinner but knew there was no other way. Marconi was a powerful man. He would have guards with him. He would be protected and hard to get close to. This was what Frank was hired to do, so this was what Frank would do.

He took his backpack and locked the door behind him. He pocketed the key and headed down to the restaurant.

It was dinner time. He planned to have a lovely meal, the

primi, the *secondi*, the *digestivo*, and a little *dolce*. During that meal, he would use the restaurant's bathroom. The entire time, he would leave the remaining squibs throughout the restaurant. Marconi would have no chance to walk away.

Each unit would be set for exactly nine in the evening, just like the two in the hotel room above. Marconi was scheduled to arrive at eight-thirty p.m. He would be sipping wine and eating pasta as the first squib blew a hole in his face.

Frank would watch from the far side of the piazza. As backup, he had his handguns. If anyone left the building before the explosion, he would shoot them.

It was genius. Now, he only needed Sarah Roberts to show up and complete his plan.

Then he had a certain minister of finance to execute.

He placed the napkin across his legs and dug into his *primi*, feeling better than he had in a long time.

Chapter 34

Sarah walked around the April 25 square four times, then settled on a park bench. There was no point in entering the restaurant before Marconi. She needed to see him go in, assess the amount of security he brought with him and watch for Frank's return. There was no doubt in her mind that Frank would come back on a different train, and when he did, he'd be angry. He would want to settle the score. Unless, of course, he really was The Cowboy.

Two black Mercedes pulled in off the main road and turned to enter the April 25 piazza. She watched from the bench, anticipation growing in her stomach.

She wore a long evening dress that covered her knees. It matched her now bright red hair, as did her new purse that held both guns. Since the change, she had gotten a lot of attention, but not because people recognized her as Sarah Roberts. She had even walked past two local Carabinieri police officers, and they looked away without recognizing her.

The one side of her hair was shaved in an eighties punk rock look. The other side remained elegant. The drastic change could be corrected over time, but she had to hide by standing out.

The Mercedes stopped in front of the Capitone Ristorante and let four men out. Then the two vehicles pulled away, drove around the piazza until they aimed for the road, and left the area, no doubt to park close by until they were summoned for a pick-up.

Leaving vehicles like that in front of the restaurant would invite unwelcome attention.

The four men wore business suits. One of them held a briefcase. The first two entered the restaurant. After a moment of examining the parking lot, the other two joined them.

Sarah checked her watch.

Eight-forty p.m.

She would give them ten minutes to settle in and then go for dinner herself. She would eye their table during a bowl of pasta and a little wine. Maybe they would eye her back. Maybe they would flirt. She entertained the idea of being invited to their table.

Won't they be surprised when I crash their party?

Chapter 35

Frank checked the time. Sam Marconi and his men had been inside for almost ten minutes. They'd been late by eight minutes, which gave him a minor coronary. If Marconi hadn't shown and Frank blew up a hotel and restaurant for nothing, he would be pretty pissed.

He had covered every base. The squibs couldn't be traced back to him during the aftermath and investigation.

He had checked into the hotel, but they wouldn't find his body in the rubble. The name he used was one of his four aliases. That ID was already burned and smoldering in a metal garbage can three blocks away.

Other than his appearance, no one could connect him to the area at all.

Just over ten minutes until the explosion.

A gorgeous woman in a long flowing dress, hair cascading down over one shoulder, entered the piazza. She walked toward the restaurant.

From where he stood, he couldn't be sure whether it was Sarah Roberts. He studied the walk, her gait. She had the same body and the same shape, but the hair was a different color—a stark red.

The woman stopped in front of the restaurant and pretended to stare at the menu on an easel display. He saw what she was doing as she slowly moved in a circle, flipping a page of the menu, watching the piazza as she went.

He backed into the shadows on the far side and focused on her face as it came into view.

Sarah Roberts.

He wanted to shout as if his soccer team had just scored a goal, but he held it in.

Sarah did not disappoint. She had shown up just before detonation. She wouldn't miss out on a meeting with The Dealer.

She entered the restaurant.

He was so giddy he almost forgot to check the time.

Both in one hit. A new record.

The building Sarah and Marconi were in would be destroyed in ten minutes.

And I've got front-row seats.

Chapter 36

A HANDSOME WAITER MET Sarah at the door and took her to a table near the back. She sat by an alcove that opened to a hallway, and the waiter obliged. The hallway was short, with stairs at the end that dropped from sight. A sign said the toilet was at the bottom of the stairs. The angle she sat gave her a frontal view of the Marconi table. None of the four men looked like the driver who had escaped earlier that day after the shooting at the internet shop.

The restaurant had two other couples at two different tables, sitting quietly, whispering to each other. All told, there were eight people, plus her and the employees. The four men who had arrived in the Mercedes were seated at one table by the front door. One of their party sat by the window; the curtain pulled back enough so that he could watch the parking lot.

Three of them had wine. The man on window duty was

drinking water.

The waiter brought her a menu and a wine list.

"I'm waiting for my date," she told the waiter. "But I would like wine to start. The house wine will be fine."

Her hand numbed.

Vivian?

"By ah the glassa?" the waiter asked. "Or bottiglia?"

"Glass," she said, smiling. Her arm numbed and jerked.

What's the emergency?

The waiter seemed to notice her hand. He paused and looked down. She shrugged and gave him a wry smile.

"Do you have a pen I could borrow?" she asked.

He pulled one from his pocket and set it on the table, then walked away to clear the dishes from one of the couples' tables.

Her right hand numbed again, then righted.

Where have you been, Vivian?

Her hand pulsed, then her arm numbed.

Right here, right now?

She looked around frantically for something to write on. The tablecloth wouldn't do. It was a burgundy cloth and not paper.

Toilet paper.

Her eye caught one of Marconi's men watching her, a frown on his face.

Shit, I caught their attention for the wrong reasons.

She grabbed her purse, picked up the waiter's pen, and headed along the hallway to the stairs. She would collect herself, chastise Vivian for such bad timing, write whatever it was Vivian wanted to say on toilet paper, and then return to her seat to deal with Marconi.

At the bottom of the stairs, the entire right side of her body numbed to the point where she couldn't remain upright. Her right foot collapsed under her. She fell hard and slid along the floor until her head was under a table with brochures by the restroom doors.

"What the fuck!" she whispered through clenched teeth. "You could be nicer about taking over my body."

She rolled onto her back, took a deep breath, then exhaled. It had a calming effect.

A tiny red light under the table blinked. Then it blinked again. The second she saw it, Vivian caused her arm to pulse twice.

What are you trying to tell me?

She leaned up closer to the light. A small black device was affixed to the underside of the table. On the side of the device, a miniature timer counted down. She checked her watch. The countdown ended in six and a half minutes at nine in the evening.

Frank De Luca. It had to be.

She hadn't seen him all day, but he wouldn't miss Marconi at this dinner. She had known he would return, but not in such a huge way.

She tossed the pen aside, got to her feet, and ran for the bathroom. At the doors that separated the men's toilet and the women's, she chose the men's room and examined it quickly.

Another black device was well hidden at the base of the toilet. Its timer was identical to the one in the hallway.

Nine p.m.

Five minutes and fifty-two seconds left.

Her stomach did back flips, and her knees weakened. A sweat broke out on her forehead. If it weren't for Vivian,

Sarah would be dead in five minutes, along with Marconi and his men.

Frank, who was probably watching from somewhere outside, would have completed his task. Frank struck her as the kind of man who strived to do the job right and ensure it was complete. That meant the entire building would be destroyed. He probably had bombs planted everywhere.

This also meant she was right. Frank wasn't The Cowboy.

She ran from the men's bathroom, even though the fear of what would happen made her want to piss her pants, and took the stairs two at a time. She walked briskly past her table, down the small length of the restaurant, and entered the kitchen.

The waiter was about to pick dishes of food up, and a chef to his right dropped basil on the food.

"Do not raise the alarm," Sarah said. "I will handle the customers. Both of you have to leave the building right now. You have to get far away."

They frowned at her.

"Perché sei nella mia cucina?" the chef said.

Maybe I do need to speak Italian—but I can't!

"There's no time. Leave by the back door."

The waiter picked up his dishes and made to walk past her, heading to the customers.

"What did your chef say?" Sarah asked.

"He asked why you were ina his kitchen."

She blocked the door and reached into her purse. A quick look at her watch gave her just over four minutes left.

The eyes of both men widened when she brought her Sig Sauer out of the purse.

"Keys to the front door?" she said to the waiter, her free hand extended. "I need the keys now."

The chef pulled them from his pocket and handed them to her, his face twisted in fear and anger.

She brought up her weapon. "Now leave this building and run as fast as possible, or I will shoot you. I'm an American, have a gun, and love to shoot people."

The dishes clattered as the waiter dropped them down on the preparation counter and turned to run, dragging the chef along with him.

"Sta per spararci," the waiter said to the chef. "È Americana!"

They hit the door and disappeared down the back alley outside. She didn't wait until the door closed before she turned around to head back to the restaurant.

"What's going on back here?" One of Marconi's men entered the kitchen.

She lowered her weapon and fired into his leg. He grunted and dropped to the floor. Even before he was completely sprawled out on the kitchen tiles, he already had a weapon out of his jacket.

In a classic soccer move, Sarah jumped in close and swung her foot, making perfect contact with the gun as it came around to bear on her. The small weapon left his hand, flew the length of the kitchen, and hit a silver freezer door on the far side.

Aaron would be proud, she thought.

She landed on both feet and shot her arm out, whacking the side of his face so hard it snapped his head sideways.

His eyes shut, and his body went limp.

She ran for the door with one glance at her watch.

Three minutes left to get the innocents out and keep the guilty in.

Shit, I'm not going to make it.

***

Frank checked his watch again. Three minutes left.

He edged along until he was down the length of the cobblestone walkway by a stone wall. At the exact moment of detonation, he would spin around the corner and be protected from any shrapnel by three hundred meters and a lot of ancient stone.

Two and a half minutes and still no sign of Marconi or Sarah leaving.

The front door opened. He leaned closer and narrowed his eyes.

A young couple he didn't recognize emerged from the restaurant. They looked over their shoulder, then ran toward a car in the piazza. Before they were lost to view, the male pulled out a cell phone and started dialing.

What's happening in there?

Could the customer be calling the police? Did Marconi recognize Sarah, or has Sarah angered Marconi?

Less than two minutes left.

The door opened again.

Frank pulled his weapon out to shoot them if it was either Sarah, Marconi, or his men.

But it was another couple. They didn't hesitate—just started running as soon as the door opened.

What the hell?

He holstered his weapon. One minute left. He edged back

into the shadows.

Nothing else moved. No one came or went.

Forty-five seconds to detonation—both Sarah and Marconi still inside.

A police siren wailed in the distance.

Too late, Frank said to himself.

The siren drew near. They were only a block or two away.

It didn't matter now. No one could deactivate his timers, and no bomb squad could stop him now.

It was too late.

Twenty seconds.

He walked backward until he leaned on the corner of the building, where he waited to fall back away from danger.

The front door of the restaurant opened.

Sarah Roberts stepped out with seconds to spare.

***

Sarah concealed her weapon and walked across the restaurant. She couldn't allow Marconi to walk out of there. He was a loose cannon. The danger he posed was the reason she came to Italy, which meant Marconi had to go. The beauty here was she had nothing to do with the bombs that would take him out.

Some people are too vile to be allowed a free pass.

At their table, she faced the remaining three men. Marconi had a glass of red wine at his lips as if the noise from the kitchen and the gunshot meant nothing to him.

"Guns on the table," she said.

Only one man slipped a hand inside his jacket, but no

guns came out.

Her weapon came out of hiding. She aimed and shot the man who had reached into his jacket in the forehead. His eyes widened briefly, then his head plopped down onto the cloth napkin, bouncing once.

The two remaining men jerked. Marconi kept the red wine glass in his hand the whole time. His remaining guard now had a hand inside his jacket but didn't know what to do.

"Pull it out slowly."

The guard did.

"Set it down."

He did, aiming it at the wall.

"Now, knock it off the table."

Marconi's man swept the gun to the floor with his arm.

"All hands on the table where I can see them."

Marconi set his wine down.

"Join your hands together. Lock them to each other across the top of the table."

"Are you Sarah Roberts?" Marconi asked, his demeanor cool like violence and death were regular companions.

She chanced a look at her watch.

Two minutes.

She nodded at the couple closest to the front door, who seemed paralyzed after watching a man get shot. "You two. Get out of here. Now!" she shouted. "Or I will have to shoot you, too."

They got up slowly, walked to the door, the male placing a hand on the female's back, and stepped outside. Marconi and his man didn't budge. They were probably waiting to make their move when the restaurant was empty.

The dead man beside Marconi bled out on the table, a

crimson circle on the tablecloth around his head.

"Your turn," she said to the other couple. "Get out of this restaurant, or you will be dead in," she checked her watch, "about a minute or so."

The man got up so fast that his chair tipped over. The woman ran for the door, banging into it on the way out, her man close behind.

Sarah started for the door, walking backward.

"Aren't you going to stay and chat?" Marconi asked. "I thought that was why you came here tonight."

She kept the Sig aimed at him as she pulled out the restaurant's keys. "Let me lock the door first. Wouldn't want to be interrupted."

Her heart was in her stomach. What if one of the timers was set a little early? What if her watch had slowed down?

The second hand ticked by the six on her watch.

Thirty seconds left.

She fired twice in Marconi's general direction and bolted for the door. She opened it hard, spun, and slammed it shut, her breath coming out in gasps. At any second, Marconi and his man would retrieve their weapons and fire at her.

She fumbled with the keys and then got the right one.

A police siren was close.

She locked the front door and turned to run. Movement inside the restaurant pulled her back.

Marconi's guard was running at the door, a gun up and ready. She fired through the glass, hitting him in the thigh. He tumbled to the floor.

When she turned around, the Carabinieri rounded the far corner and started toward the restaurant.

Five seconds left.

She ran, her gun out front.

The police were advancing too fast.

She waved her arms and shouted, "Get back!"

They didn't slow, the car's engine revving.

She stopped, took careful aim, and fired at their small car.

Instantly, the driver swerved and careened into the building to his right.

She looked over her shoulder and lifted her foot to run, but it never touched the cobblestone under it.

The building exploded behind her.

The shockwave lifted Sarah and shoved her thirty feet, where she smacked into a stone wall, falling amongst the debris and fiery shrapnel.

She moaned and opened her eyes. Chunks of stone and rock smashed the police car, breaking the windshield and denting the roof and the hood.

Pain littered her body as she slowly turned to look at the razed restaurant.

Another explosion rocked the area. More chunks of stone shot skyward. She tried to crawl away, but a chunk of debris landed on her head, just behind her ear.

Sarah's eyes closed. Her last thought was her sister's name.

Chapter 37

PARKMAN GOT ON THE exit ramp and pulled off the E45 to Umbertide in his rental. A sign pointed toward the center of town. Memories of being here a few years ago with Sarah flooded back. His eyes teared up.

If only we could go back to those days ...

He still refused to believe she was gone. Sarah's parents had called several times, but he had nothing new for them. Sarah's father, Caleb, wanted to know why he had flown to Italy. When Caleb asked for the brutal truth an hour ago, Parkman couldn't lie. Not about something so serious.

"I'm sorry, Caleb."

There was a pause.

"Parkman? What are you saying?"

"I'm in Italy to identify the body. But for the record," his voice cracked. "I don't believe she's gone."

"Parkman? Tell me you're—" Caleb dropped the phone.

Parkman waited. Scuffling noises came through. Then Caleb, wracked with sobs, said, "Tell me my little girl is okay."

Amelia wailed in the background.

Parkman didn't know what to say. "Caleb … I will meet with them in an hour. I'll update you then."

"If the unimaginable has happened, I want her body brought back here," his voice weaker now, "flown back to the States for an honorable burial. You hear me, Parkman?"

"Yes, sir. It'll happen as you wish. I won't stand for anything less."

Amelia wailed louder in the background.

"Just wait until I call you back. None of this makes sense. My gut tells me she's okay. I could be wrong—"

"Parkman … *Sarah* …" The phone clicked off.

They wanted Sarah's body shipped back to the States for a proper burial. Aaron was stuck in a jail cell. What would Aaron think when he heard? Parkman was sure Aaron would scream about how he would hunt down the people who did this when he got out of jail. He would make it his life's mission.

He parked the rental near the town center and walked into the main piazza. To his left, down a long corridor between the buildings, a roped-off area where the razed hotel and restaurant had once caught passersby's attention. Now it was a pile of stone and brick, a backhoe out front as clean-up crews worked on the rubble. According to Scott McPherson, Sarah had been here three nights ago. Now she was gone.

He shook his head and took a deep breath. He pulled out a small gold box from his pocket and opened it. Inside, he found his dwindling supply of cinnamon toothpicks. He popped one in his mouth and continued to the police station.

Once inside, he waited at the front window. An officer turned and addressed him in Italian.

"Parkman. Here to see Scott McPherson about Sarah Roberts's body."

The officer stared, his eyes probing. He paused long enough for it to be uncomfortable.

"Scott McPherson?" Parkman repeated, moving the toothpick from one side of his mouth to the other.

The uniformed Italian officer shrugged and turned away. He spoke quietly into a microphone of some sort and sat down at a desk, his back to Parkman.

What the hell is his problem?

A moment later, a door opened, and a tall, good-looking man walked through, his hand extended.

"You must be Parkman," the man said in American English.

They shook hands. "McPherson?"

The man nodded. "I wish we could've met under other circumstances."

"Me too."

"You just finished eating?"

Parkman frowned. "No. Why's that?"

"The toothpick."

"Just a habit."

It was McPherson's turn to frown. "Follow me," he said and turned toward the back of the station.

"Sarah's back here? She's not in the hospital morgue?"

McPherson stopped and glanced over his shoulder. "We need to talk first."

"About what?" Parkman asked.

"Please. You're in a foreign country. Turn off your

investigator hat and turn on your listening cap. Just follow me, and I'll explain everything."

"ID."

"Excuse me?" McPherson turned to face him.

"Your name means nothing to me. The fact that I met you at a police station is worthless. I've met the kind of men Sarah has had the misfortune of working with in the past. They've killed her in car accidents, tried to hide her in underground jails, and done all sorts of atrocities against her, all in the name of forcing her to work for them. If she's really dead, the game stops here. I want ID. I want to know who I'm talking to and why we're talking. Otherwise, a major shitstorm is coming down on this fucking charade. A price has to be paid for Sarah, and I'm the collector with a toothpick in his mouth." He flicked the pick back and forth with his tongue. "Trust me on this. So, ID."

As Parkman talked, McPherson's eyes had twitched. Then his face relaxed, and his eyes moistened.

What an act.

"You remind me of Sarah. You're a no-bullshit guy."

"I'm a no-bullshit guy. Remember that." Parkman rolled the toothpick to the other side of his mouth. From the corner of his eye, he caught the Italian officer behind the Plexiglas booth standing up and listening.

McPherson slowly pulled out his ID and handed it over for Parkman to examine. After a moment, he handed it back.

"Looks real enough. You've got my attention."

McPherson nodded, gave a half-smile, and walked away. Parkman followed him down the corridor and into a room that resembled an American interrogation room.

McPherson closed the door behind them.

"How well do you know Sarah?" McPherson asked.

"What is this?"

"Just answer the question."

"I've got one for you. Why did that cop out there give me so much attitude as soon as I mentioned your name and Sarah in the same sentence?"

"Because three nights ago, Sarah Roberts set off bombs, blew up part of their *centro storico*, and killed six people while doing it. Four in the restaurant and a couple in the hotel above. Before the bombs went off, she ran outside and fired a weapon at an advancing police vehicle. So, understandably, it's pretty tense around here." McPherson leaned his shoulder against the door. "It doesn't matter who showed up to collect Sarah's body, they aren't going to be well received."

"So she is dead? Are you confirming it?"

"Give me your cell phone."

"What?"

"Your cell phone. Hand it over."

"What the hell for?"

"Deal time. Give me the cell or stay here all day and think about it. I'll check in every once in a while to see if you're willing to give it to me."

"What the hell is going on?"

"Cell phone first, or you don't leave this building for a month or two."

Parkman pulled his phone out and tossed it to McPherson.

"Perfect." McPherson pocketed it.

"What happened to Sarah? Is she really dead?"

McPherson lowered his gaze. "I'm sorry, Parkman, but Sarah succumbed to her injuries sustained in the blast. There was nothing anyone could do for her."

Chapter 38

DARWIN USED HIS COMPUTER program to search for everything he could find on Sarah Roberts in Italy. After the news of the blast three days ago, and with the GMO conference happening tomorrow afternoon, he hadn't seen anything new on her or the actions of Marconi and his men.

His own surveillance from afar had come up empty. There were seven bodies in the rubble, according to the news. Four were in the restaurant, two from the hotel, and one unidentified female who had the misfortune of being too close to the building when it blew.

Yet three days later, none of the names had hit the media. The police were tight-lipped, releasing nothing new.

He couldn't hack into the hospital computers nor drive over and ask questions. Darwin and his family were supposed to be in their own protective custody, locked down. They had agreed to the lockdown until the GMO conference was finished and everyone had left the immediate area.

Exhausted, confused, and frustrated, he slammed a hand down on the desk.

"Damn it. Why do the good guys always have to pay the price?"

He suspected Sarah was the unidentified female outside the building when it blew up. Either that, or she was lying low until the conference.

He got up from his desk, grabbed his empty coffee cup, and headed for the kitchen.

Rosina was chopping peppers when he walked in.

"Coffee on?" Darwin asked.

"Yeah, there's still some in the pot. Anything on Sarah yet?"

"Nothing."

The knife in Rosina's hand stopped. She set it down and wiped her hands on the apron she wore.

"What are we going to do?" she asked.

Darwin poured coffee into his cup and set the pot back. "What can we do? We're officially not even here."

"If Sarah's gone, then things will work themselves out. But if she's not, is there anything we can do to help?"

"Even if there was," Darwin faced her and leaned against the counter, "what would we be doing? Exposing ourselves and risking Bradley. We can't go through what we went through before. Not with a newborn." He shook his head and then sipped from his cup.

"I know, but …"

Darwin eyed her. He set his cup on the counter and walked over to her. He put his hands on her arms and held her close. "What are you thinking, hun?"

"It's just Sarah was such a nice girl. She's been through a lot."

"I know."

"She's out there fighting this thing. I don't know. There's just something inside me that screams that we should be fighting, too. Or at least helping her if we can."

Darwin pulled her into him and hugged her tight, wrapping her head up with his arms and resting it on his chest. "I know, baby. But this is the way the world works. The eternal fight between good and evil. Evil may win, but it'll never conquer. People like us, we made it." He pulled away and held her at arm's length. "Sarah will, too. She's got a little helper in her sister." He nodded toward the ceiling. "She'll be okay."

"You don't think she's dead?"

Darwin shook his head. "No, I don't."

Rosina moved away and opened a drawer by the stove. She pulled out an Italian cookbook and set it on the cutting board.

"What's this?" Darwin asked. "Gonna show me how to make a homemade pizza or an Alfredo sauce?" He smiled and picked up his coffee.

"What if you could help Sarah without anyone knowing about it?" Rosina asked.

He paused mid-sip, lowered his cup, and stared at her. "What are you asking?"

"Just answer the question. If you could perform a task and knew it would help Sarah without anyone knowing about your involvement, would you do it? Would you leave our house, even though we're in lockdown until this conference is over?"

"It would depend on the task."

"No, it wouldn't, not if you knew you were doing it anonymously."

He thought about it as he walked to the kitchen table and sat down.

"I would. How do you feel about that?"

Rosina lifted the cookbook and walked to the table. She scooted a chair closer and sat next to him. Then she opened the cookbook. A loose piece of paper had been sandwiched between the lasagna pages.

"What's this?" Darwin asked.

"I found it on the night table in the guest room." She unfolded the paper and held it up.

"Did she leave us a note?"

Rosina shook her head. "No. Her sister did."

Darwin frowned.

"It says." Rosina cleared her throat and read the note to him.

"Oh," Darwin said. "That's some freaky shit."

"I know. I didn't know what to do with it when I first read the note."

Darwin wiped his face and rubbed his thighs a couple of times. "I got goosebumps. Wow, and that's supposedly from her dead sister?"

Rosina nodded.

"I can't do that. If I was killed—"

"Would her sister send you to your death?"

"Has she sent Sarah to her death?" Darwin countered.

Rosina looked at the note.

"Not if I'm reading this correctly. If this note is accurate, then Sarah is still alive and needs our help."

Darwin shook his head and got up. "Rosina, what she's asking is too much." He walked to the sink and poured his coffee down the drain. "I can't risk everything we've accomplished here. Even for Sarah."

"What happens if we don't help her? What would our world look like without Sarah Roberts out there?"

"I don't know, but we can't save everybody."

"We're not being asked to save everybody. Just one girl."

Darwin walked to the kitchen door and stopped to look back. "Rosina, think about Bradley."

"I have."

Darwin walked down the corridor toward his office. Over his shoulder, he said, "I can't do it. I'm sorry."

Chapter 39

Voices arguing. Men's voices. One with an Italian accent, the other two recognizable.

Parkman?

"I understand," the Italian voice said. He sounded quite angry. "The only way she leaves this hospital is in cuffs. Then it's the airport. I want her out of my city and out of my country."

"Please, you're being unreasonable," the other voice said.

Who the hell is that?

"We all know she didn't do what you think she did."

"I had officers who attended the scene," the Italian voice said. "They were shot at before the explosion. She destroyed an entire section of my ancient walled city. Don't lecture me that it's all over because Sam Marconi is dead. There are easier ways to kill a man."

"But she didn't—"

"I'm not finished," the Italian cut in. "I have a waiter and a cook who were ordered out of their kitchen at gunpoint. According to them, she said she was going to kill them. And let's not forget the destruction of the internet store earlier in the day. Witnesses there say a car raced away with your red-haired maniac here shooting at them and murdering three businessmen in suits who, as far as we know, were just stopping by to get online. She was a blonde then. This red hair was an obvious way for her to go unnoticed. I've been an officer for too many years to play in the kiddy park with the likes of you."

"Sir, with all due respect, we don't know if they attacked first. At the restaurant, she could've ordered those men out of the kitchen to save their lives, and she shot at your officers to stop their approach. She probably saved their lives."

"It is of no interest to me what your theories are. I have statements and witness accounts. I have proof, and I have bullets and shell casings that match. I also have dozens of local officers who don't want her here. I will order her shot on sight if she doesn't leave this room in cuffs and leave my country. Are we clear? Does this get through to your American way of thinking?"

"What the hell does that mean?"

"You all ride in here and shoot my city up. Then you complain when I ask you to stop. She destroys historical buildings and kills people, and you're upset with us when we ask again for you to stop. I'm done with this. We'll solve our own problems. We don't need your help anymore."

A door opened.

"McPherson," an Italian voice again, "leave as soon as

you can and take her with you or face dire consequences."

"You don't have the authority. We were asked to be here by an official who outranks you. We leave when he tells us to."

"Your choice. But this is my city. Stay out of sight. Get lost, as you Americans say." The door slammed shut.

She jolted in her bed at the sound.

"How about we play a game of fuck off? You go first."

"How mature, McPherson," Parkman said. "He can't hear you. He's already gone."

McPherson? Or Kierian?

Sarah opened her eyes.

Two men stood by the door. They both turned around at the same time. Parkman was on the left, and the other man was a dead man.

"Kierian?" Sarah said.

He raised his hands in defense.

"What?" Sarah said. "You're … alive? I thought you died in Rome."

"I can explain."

"Kierian?" Parkman asked. "I thought you said your name was McPherson?"

"It is." He looked between them. "I was using the name Kierian for so long that it just became my name."

"Who are you?" Sarah asked.

"My name is Scott McPherson. I don't work for the FBI."

"Of course, you don't," Sarah said. She looked at Parkman. "Hey, you got a gun? This guy died in Rome. Can you shoot him for me? No one will miss him. He's supposed to be dead."

Parkman moved closer.

"Whoa, whoa," Kierian said. "Let me explain."

"Start talking," Parkman said. "I warned you about this. Nobody messes with her. You lied to me once already today."

"And I explained how necessary that was."

"Start talking and start telling. She has a right to know why the Italian authorities hate her."

Kierian moved to the side of the bed. Her pulse quickened. She wanted to rip the IV from her arm and wrap the cord around his neck until his eyes popped out.

"First," she said. "Tell me about my injuries. How bad?"

"Not bad at all. Mostly bruising, cuts, and scrapes. You took a nasty hit to the head. A severe concussion, maybe swelling on the brain. Doctors induced a coma for a few days until you were in the clear."

"Am I in the clear now?"

"Looks that way."

"How long have I been out? Did the GMO conference take place?"

"You've been out all week. The conference happens tomorrow afternoon. But that doesn't matter. You're not going anywhere near that place."

"Whatever. Talk to me. Explain your ass away. Then I'm out of here."

"You're not going anywhere but to the airport."

"Fuck you. I'm not. I'm royally pissed, and I know the man who needs to pay for this. We had coffee together the other day, and now he has to die."

"You had coffee together?" Kierian asked. "Shit, I'd hate to have lunch with you."

"Stop with the routine and tell us what's going on,"

Parkman shouted.

Kierian jumped at Parkman's voice, pulled a chair over, and straddled it backward.

"I don't work for the FBI. I work with a branch of the CIA—we're almost rogue, really. We do intelligence work and gather what we can to confirm certain ambiguities the CIA has encountered. When data stored at the warehouse of the Sophia Project came across my desk, I put in for a transfer to monitor you. My old partner and I were assigned to see if there was anything to their claims."

Sarah remembered the Sophia Project clearly, and their failed attempts to recruit her until their organization was dissolved. She had no idea it would come back to haunt her.

"This was an intelligence-gathering mission," Kierian said. "You and I were supposed to meet The Cowboy in Rome and then come here. Learn what we could and report back."

"So why fake your death?"

"When you went out for a walk early that first morning in Rome, the contact who dropped the gun off the night before called me. He said Marconi's men were watching my room. We decided the best plan was to have me killed publicly so The Cowboy and the man watching the room would see it. I contacted the authorities in Rome and told them to pick you up. I would debrief you then, and we'd grab The Cowboy together. Our plan was flawless. Once we learned everything we could, we would travel back to Toronto, and your end of things was done. The trained authorities would swoop in and pick Marconi up. But no one expected you to run."

"I don't trust cops."

"Yeah, you've said that before." Kierian's face wrinkled as he winced. "But that has cost us now. You came to Umbertide, the last place on earth I thought you'd go, to the heart of the GMO conference, and killed Marconi and his henchmen. I don't know how you did it or where you got the bombs, but every cop outside this room wouldn't bat an eye if you didn't make it out of here alive."

"I didn't plant those bombs."

"Then who did? Marconi?"

"A man named Frank De Luca."

Kierian's eyes widened. His gaze swiveled to Parkman and then back to Sarah.

"You're kidding, right?"

"Why?"

"Frank De Luca is a ghost. No one has seen him in years. He works in the shadows. We have a large file on him. He's Norwegian. The only people who have ever seen him are dead. Frank is the name he's known by because most of his hits are sourced by the mafia. He's a perfectionist. He has never missed."

"And he didn't this time. His target was Marconi."

"How do you know this?" Kierian looked astounded, his mouth agape.

"I told you. We had coffee."

"Bullshit."

"Tell me about Toronto," Sarah said, changing the subject. "Was the attack on Aaron's apartment you, too?" She looked down at her body, examining her wounds. She flexed her fingers, moved her toes, and lifted her legs. A soft pain flared everywhere, but just as Kierian had said, nothing was broken. Her head ached, but that was expected after body-checking a stone wall.

"Toronto was us," Kierian admitted.

In that one sentence, Sarah decided she would kill the man she knew as Special Agent Penn Kierian.

"You motherfucker," she whispered. "You will pay for that."

"We had to up the schedule. I also wanted you to be prepared for how serious people like Marconi are. My superiors were worried I was walking an untrained civilian into trouble. I set the exercise up to show them how good you were."

"The men with blanks … that was all you and your people?"

He nodded. "All us."

"What about the man who got shot? Did he really get shot?"

"Not by me. That first shot I took was a blank. He had a blood packet in his hand connected to my gun's trigger by remote control. The gun Aaron grabbed was actually the officer's sidearm."

"So Aaron *actually* shot the man?"

"Yes, and fucked up his windshield. He just got out of the hospital the other day."

"And Aaron?" Parkman cut in. "He's stuck in jail on first-degree murder charges. Is that why it's so hush-hush?"

"Yes. Those charges are to keep him protected while we are over here. As soon as we land in Toronto, all charges will be expunged from the record as if they didn't happen. Not even an arrest record. But nothing changes until Sarah is on Canadian soil."

"So that's why Agent Hanover couldn't find anything on

an agent named Kierian," Parkman said.

"Wow, you've really done a number on my family and me." Sarah rolled her head across the pillow. "Get me a phone. I gotta call home."

Parkman padded his pockets. "Oh yeah." He looked at Kierian. "You took my cell."

"I'm afraid no one can go anywhere or call anyone until this thing is over."

"So you're going to let Aaron rot in jail, and my parents think I'm in trouble, or worse?"

"Sarah," Parkman stepped closer. "They know I'm here to identify your body. They think you're dead."

Her eyes welled up in tears. "Kierian, you better fix this. Right fucking now. Or I will."

"I'm afraid I can't. A man like Frank De Luca has an army working for him. Nothing changes until after the weekend. This GMO conference has to happen as planned. The authorities have a police guard placed outside your door. You can't leave this room until Monday. It's for your own good. Especially knowing that Frank De Luca is local."

Sarah pulled the IV out of her arm and yanked the white bed sheet off. "Because Frank is in town; I need out of here."

"Sarah, you can't," Kierian got up and stood in front of her. Parkman moved in.

"Everyone relax," Sarah shouted. "Kierian, you've got him to ID my body." She pointed at Parkman. "Declare me dead. My parents already think so, anyway. Then I go after Frank and the man who hired him."

"You know who hired Frank?"

"Yes, I do." She wavered on her feet, dizzy, her legs weak from being in bed for so long. She held the bed's rail for a second until it passed.

"You okay, Sarah?" Parkman asked, stepping closer.

"Yes, just got up too fast."

"Who hired De Luca?" Kierian asked.

"None of your business. Get me out of here, and I'll tell you. Then I can go after De Luca, and you can go after his boss."

"No deal. Even if I liked the idea, even if I saw great success with it, I couldn't agree to it." He looked at Parkman. "You heard the senior officer of the state police. He said he would send out a 'shoot on sight' order if Sarah leaves this room." He looked back at Sarah. "It would be a death sentence for you to leave this room. The funeral your parents are no doubt planning will actually have a body for the coffin if you go out that door."

"I'll take my chances," Sarah said.

"Then you'll die."

"You've fucked with me since we met, Kierian. You've lied to me, had Aaron arrested, and now my parents think I'm dead, all because of you. Stand in my way, please. Try to stop me." She stepped toward him. "So I can hurt you bad. Because right now, I can't think of anything I would like more than to rip your face off and use the skin as a lampshade."

"Sarah, that's creepy," Parkman said.

"I know, sorry. Couldn't think of anything worse right now."

"Who fucked up your hair?" Parkman asked. "You look like you belong on the 'People of Wal-Mart' website."

"Nice. Thanks, dickweed."

"Love you, too, Sarah."

She smiled at him and tapped his shoulder more for support to keep standing.

"Sarah, think about this," Kierian said as he stepped backward.

A second wave of dizziness swept over her. She teetered and then stumbled. Before hitting the hospital floor, Parkman's arms came in fast and eased her down.

Then she was out.

Chapter 40

DARWIN ENTERED A SIDE door of the Umbertide hospital. Vivian's note, authored by Sarah, had asked him to do several things. After talking with his wife, she had convinced him. They could never forgive themselves if something happened to Sarah because they failed to act when she needed them the most.

Whether it was the dead sister Sarah had talked about or Sarah herself, the note had said to come at five sharp in the morning and cause a distraction on the third floor. Just enough to pull the police officer from the door.

Darwin reached the third floor without being stopped by the minimal hospital staff at this early hour. He had worn one of his many wigs and felt his disguise would never reveal who he really was if they had him on camera.

A guard outside the hospital room the note referred to sat reading a newspaper, a small coffee cup on the floor beside his chair.

Darwin took his jacket off and limped down the hall. He wore shorts and a tank top, so his multiple scars were exposed.

When he was fifteen feet away, the officer looked up.

"Tutto bene?" the cop asked.

"No," Darwin said, a pained expression on his face. "I'm not okay." He leaned against the wall and breathed heavily. Then he continued, waving the cop to help support him. "I need your help."

The cop looked up and down the empty hallway and then got to his feet. Darwin wrapped an arm around his shoulders. Together, they walked another fifteen feet to the nurses' station.

"Thank you so much for your help," Darwin said. "But there's no nurse here."

"She stepped away but said she'd be back in a moment."

"I'm in a lot of pain. You think you could ring them or go get them?"

The cop looked back at the door he had been guarding. Then he checked his watch.

"Are you hospital security?" Darwin asked.

The cop shook his head. "Just watching a door."

"It's not even six in the morning. Nothing's going to happen. I'll watch the door for you. Please, just get a nurse." He winced and pretended to fall. "Hurry."

"Okay, okay, sit down then. I'll be right back."

The cop turned a corner and ran down the hall leading the other way.

The door he had been guarding clicked open.

***

Sarah's internal clock woke her half an hour before five in the morning. She quietly got up, pulled out her IV, and found her dirty clothes. Beside that sat the jeans and sweater Parkman had bought for when she left the hospital.

She dressed slowly, favoring her bruises. Amazed nothing had broken, the doctor said she must've blacked out momentarily before she landed, making her body limp enough to hit the wall and ground without snapping anything. The only unfortunate part was her head, which he had to stitch.

Parkman had stayed with her, had dinner, and then was allowed to go with Kierian to another room where he would sleep after he had agreed to confidentiality regarding Sarah. Kierian even made Parkman sign a document that no one would know about Kierian's or Sarah's condition until after the weekend.

Sarah used the bathroom and washed her face. After the men had left her alone last night, Vivian had come. The message told her where to go and what to do. Some of it was confusing, but Sarah was prepared to do what she was told and attend the GMO conference.

Nothing and no one would stop her from finishing this her way. Not even the guard outside her door.

Vivian said the guard would be gone for one minute at 5:03 a.m. exactly.

Sarah waited inside the room. There were voices in the hall. Two men were talking.

What did Kierian do with my guns?

Maybe the Italian authorities took her weapons. It didn't

matter. Vivian said she had taken care of that.

It had been so good to hear from Vivian again.

5:03 a.m.

She opened the door slowly. The cop's seat was empty, a small coffee cup on the floor beside a folded newspaper.

She stepped out and looked both ways.

A man in shorts and a tank top stood by the nurses' station, watching her, a jacket draped over his arm.

He leaned down and pulled his arm back. Then he tossed his jacket down the hallway. It slid along the floor and stopped three feet in front of her.

"Take it," he whispered.

She recognized the voice but couldn't tell who he was right away.

"It's Darwin," the man said. "Your sister asked me to be here."

Sarah's eyes widened. "How?"

"Long story. Maybe later. Just take my jacket and get out of here before the cop gets back."

"I … I'm sorry you got involved."

"I'm not. Now get out of here."

Footsteps beat down the hall from around the corner on the other side of Darwin. She didn't need any more prodding.

She picked up the jacket and ran the other way, slipping it on. Muscles ached, joints protested, but Sarah was past caring.

At the exit door three levels below, Sarah lifted the jacket collar and walked away from the hospital with Vivian's note tucked in her pants pocket.

Something hard bumped her ribs.

She reached into the jacket pocket and found a gun. In

the other pocket, extra rounds.

She almost wept at his kindness.

An inside pocket held a pair of scissors and a plastic baggie of dog food.

How could Darwin know what I needed? Vivian? But how the hell did Vivian talk to him?

***

Sarah disappeared around the corner at the same second the cop showed up beside Darwin.

"This nurse here can help you," he said. He searched the hall by the door where his empty chair sat.

"Everything's fine," Darwin said. "Not a peep."

The cop nodded and smiled. He walked by Darwin, headed for the chair and his coffee cup on the floor.

"What seems to be the trouble?" the nurse asked.

"Lots of pain. Look at these scars," he showed her his arms. "Everything hurts."

"What happened?"

"Long story."

"But it looks like everything healed a long time ago."

"I know, but it still hurts."

"What room are you in?" the nurse asked.

"I'm not in any room." Darwin checked the cop. He was back in his chair, a newspaper in hand.

"I'm sorry, sir, but you must register and check in downstairs."

"Oh, I didn't know. Where do I go?"

"This way," the nurse pointed the way the cop had gone. "Down the elevator and register at the main desk. They'll have someone attend to you there."

"Thanks very much."

Darwin limped around the corner and started down the hall. He got on the elevator, rode to the first floor, and left the hospital. On the way by the dumpster, he pulled the long-haired wig off and tossed it away.

I'll see you at one in the afternoon, Sarah.

He smiled to himself at how much fun it was being back in the game, even if it was only for a little while.

Chapter 41

SARAH WALKED AS THE sun rose. Antico Caffè opened at six. She stopped there to fill her stomach with cornetti and two cappuccinos. Then she headed along the main road that led out of town, per Vivian's instructions.

She steeled herself against what she had to do. There was no other way. She kept her head down and hid most of her red hair under the back of the jacket. At this early hour, traffic was light, but a police car could happen by any time. She could not be apprehended again. Arresting her now would cause the murder of those two Italian ministers who were coming to speak at the GMO conference.

She passed the train station and kept walking. A concrete path had been built to the right of the road. She followed it, per Vivian's instructions, until it dropped to the right and went under the train bridge. After crossing the Tiber River, she came to a T in the road. To her right sat a broken-down tobacco farm that had been abandoned years ago. The tiled roof of the fieldstone structure had collapsed a decade or two before. Birds flew in and out of the roof.

This side road was even quieter than the one with the concrete walkway. Only one car had passed her since she crossed over the river. A red sign was posted on the side of the building in Italian, no doubt warning that the structure was dangerous and unfit for living in. She couldn't read the words but assumed one of them said condemned.

Without a car in sight, she walked onto the property and headed for the back of the main building. There were three buildings on the land. The main house had some form of a garage with wide open archways, and the other appeared to be a building once used for livestock. At the rear of the house, she couldn't see the road. That meant if anyone came by, they wouldn't see her.

The sun wasn't too hot this early yet, but sweat beaded on her forehead nonetheless. Her hands shook, and her stomach rolled at what Vivian had told her she would find in the cellar of this abandoned house.

She said a silent prayer, checked that Darwin's gun was loaded and ready, and tried the back door. It didn't budge. She pushed harder. Nothing. She examined the exterior to see where it was caught. Nails everywhere. Someone didn't want anyone else getting in for a long time.

Sarah stepped back and ran at the door, lifted her right foot, and kicked just as Aaron had taught her. After hitting the door, she landed hard, almost lost her balance, and ended up on her knees. She breathed in deeply, trying to collect herself, old injuries protesting. The hit on the door had rattled her. After playing punching bag to a stone wall three days ago, she wasn't up to body checking a door. Her foot would have to do.

She got up and looked around. Maybe there was something she could use to break in, but a quick survey of the immediate area found nothing. Short of heading over to the garage and trying to locate a rock, she would have to keep kicking at the door. Even if she found a rock, it would mean risking exposure to the road, which she couldn't afford.

If what Vivian said was true, which Sarah had no doubt, then be found on this property would see her in jail for many years to come.

She gave the wooden door front kick after front kick until it started to weaken. She changed feet, changed position, and even kicked facing away from it, her foot coming from behind.

Finally, the door cracked. She pulled on the wood and yanked a piece out. After that, it got easier. In fifteen minutes, she was able to slip inside the house sideways.

The inside was ruined. Weeds, straw, and bits of abandoned machinery lay scattered throughout the building. It was dank and smelled of old urine. But there was something else mixed in with the smell.

The putrid smell of something dead.

She gagged briefly, swallowed, got herself under control, and started walking across the floor, testing it routinely for safety. With the windows boarded up, only bits of sunlight came through cracks in the walls. The roof had collapsed, but that was on the second floor, leaving this area somewhat dark. To the far right, a stairwell led up. Sunlight came down the stairs, illuminating them as if a spotlight had been suspended at the top.

Sarah headed that way. The stairs to the cellar were probably under the stairs to the second floor.

Halfway across the main floor, she stopped at the sound of a car going by slowly outside. She waited, breathing quietly, listening. The vehicle continued along the road and faded in the distance.

She took another step, tested it, and then took another. A couple of times, the cracking under her feet made her think she would fall right through the floor.

Thump.

As she neared the top of the stairs, something made a noise in the cellar. Hair lifted on the back of her neck, and goosebumps rose as she pulled the weapon so fast she almost dropped it.

The main floor remained empty, but something was in the cellar. She waited and listened, the gun aimed down the stairs.

She edged closer to the stairs and looked down. It was completely dark, a murky blackness she had no desire to explore, but according to Vivian, she had to.

Shit. Isn't there another way, Vivian?

She moved to the top step.

"I've got a gun," she yelled down. Then she realized how weak that sounded.

Dealing with a tough guy and a knife or a gun was one thing. An enemy she understood and could fight. Dealing with an unknown in a basement of an abandoned building gave her the creeps.

Something scurried in the dark below.

Fear turned to anger. "Okay, I'm coming down. Piss me off, and I'll shoot first, talk later."

She took the first step.

More scurrying.

Probably mice.

She took another step.

Or rats. She shuddered. *I fucking hate rats.*

She descended the steps into the darkness one at a time, the gun extended, her arms rigid.

Chapter 42

PARKMAN STEPPED OFF THE elevator at the same time Kierian walked by the open elevator doors. He held two Americanos and two croissants in his hand.

"You're here early," Parkman said.

Kierian slowed and then stopped. "What, no good morning?"

"Is it?"

"Is it what?"

"A good morning?"

Kierian gave him a quick shake of the head. "You and Sarah are so much alike."

"I don't think that's all there is to it."

"What is it then?" Kierian asked.

"We're real people. Try it sometime. You might like it. That coffee for Sarah?"

"Yup."

"Let's go."

They walked the corridor together. At the door, the police guard didn't check ID. It was the same guard on the night shift since Sarah had arrived.

"Quiet night?" Kierian asked.

The guard nodded, his eyes bloodshot. "Tutto bene?" *Is everything okay?*

"Great."

Kierian knocked. Parkman held back and waited behind him. After a moment, Kierian knocked again.

The guard frowned. "Maybe she's still sleeping."

Kierian grabbed the door handle and twisted it. As he opened the door, he said, "Sarah, we're coming in. Hope you're decent."

The door opened all the way. Parkman followed Kierian inside.

"She's gone," Parkman said.

"What happened?" Kierian turned to the guard, who had a stunned look on his face.

The guard ran to the window. It was locked. He spewed a barrage of Italian, probably to explain his ineptness.

Parkman's stomach dropped thinking about Sarah out there somewhere alone with the Italian authorities hunting her.

This did not look good.

Kierian handed him the second Americano as Sarah wouldn't be drinking it. Parkman checked the closet where he had placed the new clothes yesterday.

They were gone.

"What's he saying?" Parkman asked.

"He's saying he saw nothing. Sarah did not leave the

room."

"He may want to check his eyes again. She's not here."

"Wait, he's saying something about a man in pain."

"A man in pain?"

Parkman ate both croissants without offering one to either man as he waited, listening to the Italian officer explain himself to Kierian. He picked up the odd word, but not enough to understand everything he was saying.

He knew Sarah too well. She wouldn't sit in a hospital room and wait to be shipped back to the States like a piece of cargo. No, she would go after who screwed with her, and Vivian would help. However, she pulled this escape off; he knew it would remain a mystery to these men by the confounded looks on their faces.

Kierian turned to him. "He said around five in the morning, a man showed up complaining of pain. He helped him walk to the nurses' station and called a nurse for the man."

"How did he call a nurse?" Parkman asked. "Did he shout or use a telephone?"

Kierian asked the guard. He turned back to Parkman. "He said he walked down the corridor about thirty yards, got her, and then returned. No longer than a minute."

"Sarah only needs five seconds."

The door swung open, and the senior officer from yesterday stepped inside.

Antonio Delarusso.

His dark features were lined with gray hair and wrinkled skin from either too much smoking or too much sun. He had bags under his eyes. A thick mustache kept his mouth hidden. Only the man's bottom lip showed when he talked.

"What's happening here?" he asked in English.

"Sarah's gone," Kierian said.

The officer moved sideways and looked past Kierian's shoulder at the empty bed. He didn't meet Parkman's eyes.

"And you are about to tell me the plane she is on?"

Kierian shook his head slowly.

"Then I will tell you that her safety isn't my concern."

"Hey," Parkman yelled and got off the bed. The guard by the window edged closer, but Parkman gave him a hard stare, and the guard stopped moving. "Her safety had better be of utmost concern to you, or I'll have your badge. A statement like that sounds like a death threat, which is still illegal in this country."

"I'm merely explaining that I can't protect her if she is out there."

"Bullshit. If something happens to her with your trigger-happy fuckups, I'll call your name."

"Are you threatening me now?"

"No. I'm merely explaining that if something happens to her, you're not above the law."

"I will send out an order to have her picked up. I can't control my men if she resists arrest."

"Who is in charge?" Parkman asked as he walked across to stand in front of the senior officer.

"I am."

"Exactly. And don't your men take orders from you."

"They do."

"Then control your men. If something happens to Sarah, it's on you, and you're the man I'll come to for an explanation. In the meantime, I'm leaving. I'll find her first, and then you won't have to worry about killing her."

His anger at the injustices Sarah always faced with cops riled him. How come they didn't just shut up and help her? How come they always had to suspect her as the bad one? Was it jealousy because she got the job done when they couldn't?

He hit the door as he left the room.

He had to find Sarah before they did. It was the only way to guarantee she would live.

But he suspected Delarusso had a different agenda, one he wasn't letting anyone else in on.

Chapter 43

THE DARKNESS IN THE cellar of the abandoned building at the bottom of the stairs was almost absolute, the smell overwhelming.

"Anyone there?" Sarah asked.

More scurrying came from somewhere in the darkness ahead.

She had to find a way to see. The extra ammunition Darwin had given her would work. She raised the gun and fired once into the floor above. A large hole was punched in the wood, offering a circular spotlight on the floor five feet in front of her.

Even though the report of the weapon had been loud in the confined space, the scurrying was easily audible as it had intensified. She fired again, not too worried about being heard by passing cars. Then once more, making a path of spotlights to see where she was headed.

A chunky rat with a long thick tail ran by one lighted hole on the dirty cellar floor. Another rat followed.

"Shit."

She tried to hold her breath, but it was impossible. She gagged again at the smell of rotting flesh.

In the light that beamed down from the third hole, the edge of a shoe was visible. She moved closer and fired one more time directly above the shoe.

When this bullet punched a hole in the floor, an entire chunk of wood snapped out of place and fell to the cellar floor, and a cloud of dust and pungent odor rose.

She leaned over and held her stomach, sure she'd vomit. After not throwing up, she turned around and slipped the gun into the jacket's pocket.

A man lay stretched out on his back. Beside him, according to Vivian's note, lay his wife on her side, most of her face missing. The left side of her jaw and cheek were gone. The bullet that killed her went so deep her spinal cord was visible.

The man's wounds were harder to see. Four small bullet holes were grouped together on the chest of his denim coveralls.

Sarah thanked God this farming couple didn't have any children, or they would be lying here with them.

Vivian had explained there was nothing Sarah could've done for them. She was preparing for the restaurant that fateful evening when this couple was taken from their home and brought here to be murdered.

This was the couple who owned the cornfields at the farm where the GMO conference was being held later that day. Someone was taking their place. Someone with an altogether different plan.

Sarah could do something about that.

The bodies had been dead for a few days. The skin was bloated and gaseous. Rigor had set in and was already relaxing as the muscles and tendons all let go. The bodily fluids had settled to the lowest points, and their wastes had vacated days ago.

She looked away, took in a rancid breath, and turned back to the male's body. Then she pulled the scissors out and started cutting the bottom pant leg off the man's coveralls where no blood or bodily fluids had marked it. After she cut out a strip the size of an average ruler, she pulled back, crossed her chest, and walked briskly across the floor, stuffing the scissors and the denim in her pocket.

At the bottom of the stairs, she took one more look over her shoulder and started up. Halfway up the stone steps, someone moved into the light above.

"Hello?" a man said in a British accent.

Sarah jumped and fumbled for her gun.

"What's that smell?" the man asked.

Sarah yanked the gun out and kept it hidden by her leg.

"What are you doing here?" she asked.

"I was on my mountain bike passing by this house when I thought I heard gunshots. I stopped because I was surprised they were hunting back here already. Then I heard more shots and saw the back door there had been smashed up. I just called the police."

Shit!

She brought the weapon up. "Bad choice." She ascended the stairs. "You should've kept peddling by."

He raised his hands and stepped back. "Whoa, I didn't

see anything."

"That's right; you didn't. And you didn't see me, either."

He shook his head violently, his eyes wide. "I didn't see you," he agreed. Then he turned his head and looked away from her.

"You're going to walk away from this building and keep walking. When you get to where you're staying, you'll thank your lucky stars I didn't shoot you. Because I could, and no one would ever know."

He nodded in an exaggerated manner.

"Let's go," she said. "Walk to the door."

She followed him, crisscrossing around the new holes in the floor, breathing deeper now that she was farther from the bodies.

He stepped through the small opening at the door, and she followed, gun first, to maintain her aim on him.

"Now start walking."

"I can't use my bike?"

"No. I'm confiscating it. You're walking."

He backed away. At the corner of the building, he lowered his hands, turned around, and ran.

Sarah got on his bike and pedaled the other way. It wasn't until she crossed the Tiber River, located the farmer's house, and started down his private road that she realized she hadn't grabbed the guy's cell phone.

Shit, I could've called in. They're going to think I killed those people.

Chapter 44

Kierian sat in the back seat of the police car en route to an abandoned farmhouse on the outskirts of Umbertide.

A British man called and said a fiery red-haired American woman had held him at gunpoint and stolen his mountain bike. The senior officer, Delarusso, who was tasked to head the security of the GMO conference and wanted Sarah out of his city, asked Kierian to come along because Parkman had already left on his own.

They drove over a bridge, sirens blaring and raced by an empty field.

"What used to be here?" Kierian asked.

"Tobacco," the officer in the passenger seat said. Kierian had forgotten his name. "This whole area was big for tobacco in the past. Farmers used to make good money in this region with it."

They turned at a T in the road and, a moment later, pulled

into an abandoned farmhouse where three buildings sat in disarray.

All three men jumped out as a man wearing cycling pants ran toward them.

"I can't believe this woman," the man said.

"Please," Kierian said. "Start at the beginning."

"I heard shots, so I pulled off the road. I came to the back here and saw that broken door." He pointed. "I couldn't see any hunters, so I slipped inside the door to have a look around. I know, maybe I shouldn't have, but I'm a curious sort."

"When you say shots, do you mean gunshots?"

He nodded. "Yes. It was a red-haired American woman."

Kierian and Delarusso exchanged a look.

"She pulled a weapon on me and said I was lucky she didn't just shoot me and walk away. Something like that. The balls on this woman."

"Sounds like Sarah," Delarusso said.

"Also, there's this smell …" The British man shook his head and waved a hand in front of his nose.

"What do you think she was shooting at?" Kierian asked.

"Well, whatever it was, it's in the cellar because that's where I found her."

The cop who rode along with them ran over to the car and retrieved a mag light.

The three men followed the Brit into the house and across the floor, listening to him rant about how people didn't have as many guns in Britain. Kierian didn't want to listen to the gun debate.

The Brit pointed down the stairs while covering his nose. "She was down there when I got here, but I didn't go down. I didn't have a light, and that smell …"

Kierian followed the officer with the flashlight. At the bottom of the stairs, rats scurried away. By the time they had moved five feet into the basement, both men saw the bodies.

Delarusso came up behind them. "Shots fired," he said. "Two dead bodies here. A witness placed Sarah at the scene. Could you even attempt to explain this one away?"

Kierian was speechless.

"Hey," the Brit yelled from the top of the stairs. "Doesn't anybody want to take a description of my mountain bike? She stole it. That's why I called you lot."

Chapter 45

SARAH RODE HARD ALONG the private drive of the farm. On her left, the train tracks ran parallel to the driveway. They gave her an idea for escape if she needed one later. To her right, the farmer's field sprawled out until it touched the banks of the Tiber. A temporary stage had already been set up for today's conference. The old rustico farmhouse came up on the right. She eased onto the gravel driveway and stopped pedaling, letting the bike glide down the slight decline as she approached the house, watching everywhere for movement.

At the end of the driveway, she steered to the brush on the side and rolled the bike out of view. Before doing anything else, she pulled out the denim patch from the man who had owned this property from her pocket and then the packet of dog food.

It didn't look like anyone was here this early. The only sounds were birds flitting in the trees and the distant roar of the highway.

According to Vivian, the farmer's dog was left on the property without food or water.

Sarah walked out of the brush and headed around to the back of the house. She leaned against the stone wall at the corner and took a moment to breathe. Her nerves were still zinging from the dead couple in the cellar. Also, at any moment, their dog would act aggressively toward her to guard their property.

She turned the corner slowly. A small lawn on this side of the house needed tending. Large rocks mixed with bricks lay in a pile to her left, surrounding two walls that hadn't entirely fallen down. Something had collapsed here years ago, and no one had bothered to rebuild or clean it up.

She walked onto the lawn and examined the back wall of the house, looking at each window for movement.

Below what looked like the kitchen window was an old wooden door. The cellar of this house was ground level. She walked over to the door and tried the handle.

It opened. She cautiously stepped inside, holding the plastic baggie of dog food in front of her.

"Here, boy," she whispered.

Once inside the gloom of the dusty cellar, she closed the door behind her. At the back of the cavernous room were a row of windows and another wooden door. The windows allowed enough light for her to see the entire room.

To her right was an extensive workbench. Tools hung suspended from the thick wooden beams crisscrossing the roof. Cobwebs hung in the less-used spaces above her head.

The workbench was covered with tiny boxes of nails, screws, hoses, and other items the farmer had been using before his untimely death.

She heard the low growl as she turned for the door to her right.

She stopped moving, her eyes roaming the floors.

The growl came again.

Of course. That's how the killers missed her. She's stealthy.

The dog had been in the cellar when they came.

"Hey, Betsy," Sarah said. She had no idea why an Italian farmer would call their dog Betsy, but that's what Vivian said the dog's name was.

"Betsy, it's okay."

The dog would probably respond better to Italian. She tried to remember a few words.

"Bene," she said, recalling that meant *good.*

"Bene, bene," she repeated.

The growl moved closer until the dog stepped from behind the counter near the door that led upstairs.

The dog was hungry, scared, and lonely.

"It's okay," she said in her softest, loving voice.

She opened the baggie all the way, pulled a few morsels out, and tossed them at the dog.

"It's okay, Betsy. Go ahead. Have something to eat."

Betsy, a large German shepherd, looked at the food and then back at Sarah.

"It's okay," Sarah said again. Two cappuccinos, two dead bodies, and now two minutes to appease a huge dog or get eaten. Her hands trembled at the notion.

She considered pulling the gun and keeping it handy. She could deal with angry men, but a pissed-off guard dog was something else entirely.

She tossed more food, hoping Betsy would warm to her.

Betsy looked down again, but this time lowered her snout and sniffed the food. One more glance at Sarah and Betsy ate the pieces.

Sarah tossed more. Betsy ate all of it.

Then Sarah tossed food closer to her feet.

"Come on. You can do it."

Betsy moved closer and ate again.

Sarah repeated the process until the dog was four feet away. Then she took the denim patch and held it out toward the dog. After the ritual hesitation, Betsy edged close enough to sniff the patch.

The dog's eyes changed subtly as she relaxed in her alpha's scent.

"Good girl," Sarah said softly as she dumped the rest of the dog food onto the floor.

Betsy ate ravenously as Sarah moved to her side and ran her hand along the dog's back. Betsy looked up when the food was gone and tried to lick Sarah's face.

She giggled and reared back to avoid the slobbery pink wetness.

"Oh, Betsy, I'm so sorry your owner was taken from you."

The dog was so close Sarah hugged her. The animal leaned into her, wanting to be held, and consoled.

But it was time to get into position.

"Okay, Betsy. You need water. Come on upstairs before anybody arrives. We haven't got much time."

Sarah got to her feet slowly. She opened the door to the upstairs and looked around the corner. As Vivian told her, stone steps led up to the kitchen.

"Come on," she whispered with a wave of her hand. The dog's tail wagged for the first time as she trotted over, passed through Sarah's legs, and headed up the stairs.

"Betsy, wait."

The dog got to the top and turned the corner. Sarah followed, but before turning the corner, she drew her weapon.

Inside the kitchen, the dog sat by the old fireplace beside her food dishes. Sarah swept the gun left, then right, but no one else was in the room.

The fridge was to her left, and the counter lined the back wall. Everything was rustic, old, and withered, but maybe that was a style the farmers preferred. Pots and pans hung from a wire square suspended from the ceiling. Cloves of garlic were tied to the edge of the wire square, as well as onions.

Sarah grabbed the silver water dish and filled it in the sink. When she set it back down, Betsy lapped it up with vigor.

Sarah walked through the kitchen to an alcove to look into the dining and living room. It was also empty. As far as she could tell, she and Betsy were the only ones in the house.

She dropped the gun in the jacket pocket.

"I have to see the bathroom. Then we hide until later, okay?"

Betsy looked up at Sarah, then dropped her head and continued licking the water.

"You stay here, then."

Sarah walked the length of the dining room and the living room, past the couches and doors that led to bedrooms on her right until she got to the last door at the end of the house.

Inside, she found a large bathroom that was a waste of space. The shower, washing machine, toilet, and tub didn't take up even half of the room. She walked around it in a circle and looked out each of the three windows.

The third window, by the toilet, had the best view of the temporary stage set up for the conference.

This was the window the sniper would come to. She was sure of it.

She headed for the kitchen.

Betsy was gone.

"Shit," she mumbled. "Betsy."

Nothing.

A vehicle approached from outside. Then another.

She had to hide. She had to be inside when the sniper arrived.

According to Vivian, the only room where she was supposed to be safe was the sunken living room.

That couldn't be the main living room. She had just walked through it twice.

A door opened downstairs. Metal clanged against something.

She ran out of the kitchen and tried the first door on her right.

Someone was coming up the stairs.

The door opened onto a square room that was larger than an average bedroom. Inside were a small writing desk and a couple of lounge chairs.

Three steps dropped down into the room.

The sunken living room.

She jumped in and closed the door behind her just as

whoever was coming up the steps entered the kitchen.

The door had a wooden latch that secured it from the inside. She brought the handle down slowly and locked the door.

She backed away quietly, moved to the far corner, and sat in one of the lounge chairs.

Someone pushed on the door from the outside. She held her breath and didn't make a sound. They pushed again, trying harder. The door didn't budge.

They gave up and walked away.

Sarah leaned back and rested in the chair, knowing she had at least two hours before the sniper would attempt to take his fatal shot.

She closed her eyes and thought about Betsy, hoping she was okay wherever she had gone. She listened to whoever was in the house and waited, preparing herself for what she had to do as hundreds of people began to gather for the conference outside the farmhouse amidst heightened security.

Chapter 46

PARKMAN STOOD BESIDE KIERIAN in the farmer's field. They were directly between the house and the temporary stage set up for the conference.

"You can't be serious," he said. "They've actually got a 'shoot on sight' order out for Sarah now?"

Kierian nodded. "They wouldn't listen to me."

"Have they identified the bodies in the cellar of that abandoned building yet?"

Kierian shook his head. "No."

"You said that time of death was not this morning when that British guy heard the shots and witnessed Sarah leaving the building. Your words were, with the condition the bodies were in, there was no way Sarah did that. They had to be dead for twenty-four to thirty-six hours, and Sarah was in a drug-induced sleep at that time in the hospital. Do you remember saying that?"

Kierian looked around and raised his hand to pat Parkman's shoulder. "Look, calm down. We'll find—"

"Don't touch me."

Kierian dropped his hand.

"This isn't the time to calm down," Parkman said. "Sarah's out there somewhere, and she's alone with an army of cops aching to shoot her. The odds aren't good, and they aren't fair. Didn't her version of the story make sense to anybody?"

His toothpick supply was out. He hadn't been able to locate any since arriving in Umbertide. It was times like this that he really needed one.

Kierian stared at Parkman sideways. "There are some who suggest that Frank De Luca isn't even a real person. How the hell could Sarah meet the man for coffee and still be alive? You have to admit, that's science fiction to the Italian authorities."

Parkman leaned in close. He wrapped a hand around Kierian's tie and yanked. "She's still alive because she's Sarah. If she says she met De Luca, then she did. End of story. Once you start believing her, she starts trusting you. That's how this shit works." He released Kierian's tie and stepped back. "Something's wrong. In a civilized country, they don't order someone shot when there's enough doubt. They bring her in and question her. Even charge her. They don't just kill her. Whoever's pulling the strings has been compromised."

"Parkman, be careful. You're talking Delarusso here, the head of state police." He lowered his voice. "Watch what you say when in his lair."

"You think I fuckin' care about whose lair I'm in?

Corruption is in every police force, and I won't let anyone hurt Sarah because of a payoff. She's too important."

Kierian stepped away. They were surrounded by hundreds of people who had gathered in the field, setting up lawn chairs, some with coolers, others with small cases of beer. If he hadn't known any better, he would've thought this was a concert of some sort.

A wall of blue uniforms surrounded the perimeter of the field. They thickened at the stage area where Delarusso stood.

Local and state police worked together to ensure this event went smoothly. The health and environment ministers had increased their security recently after the assassination of the minister of agriculture. Even though Sam "The Dealer" Marconi had claimed responsibility for that murder, and he was dead now, no one was taking security lightly.

A line of black vehicles entered the field. They snaked through the land on the makeshift tractor road and weaved through men in blue until the row of cars stopped by the stage.

"Any idea where Sarah would go?" Kierian asked.

"None. If I did, I would be there and not here."

Kierian nodded. "This is on me, isn't it?"

Parkman didn't respond.

Men exited the vehicles behind the stage and walked in a line up the few steps and onto the platform where speech after speech was about to be recorded in Italian history.

"All I can say about who's at fault is we better get to Sarah before these assholes do because if they just shoot her as they're ordered to, I'm probably never going to leave Italy."

"Why not?" Kierian frowned.

"When I locate the shooter, I will kill him, and as he dies, my face will be the last thing he sees. The last thing he hears will be me telling him that I did it for Sarah."

"Now, Parkman."

He turned to face Kierian. "You think I can go back to the States and face her parents after all the shit Sarah and I've been through and tell them that an Italian police officer killed their daughter? No way."

"Cooler heads prevail—"

"Kierian, please, just stop talking. It's you, and the idiots you work for that brought Sarah into this. You need to get her out. In the meantime, anything you say or do is only pissing me off right now. I'm going to find Sarah. I suggest you get a head start. Find her first and keep her safe."

Kierian backed away and wandered off through the crowd.

A man on stage came up to the microphone and tapped it twice. He said in English, "Testing, testing, testing."

A moment later, another man approached the microphone and thanked everyone for coming. He also spoke in English and then in Italian.

"We are gathered here today in a cornfield to talk about GMOs and how they are destroying the planet," the man said. "Ironically, this farmer was almost put out of business because of a lawsuit that began due to cross-pollination."

Parkman tuned the man out as he moved back through the crowd, headed toward the side. He wanted a better view of the entire field. This much police presence meant someone somewhere felt there was still a credible threat to the members on stage. If anything happened, Parkman wanted a good line of sight.

"We need to win this war on GMOs," the man continued. "We demand transparency regarding the testing of genetically modified foods, and we demand labels, but most of all, we want an all-out ban on GMOs in Italy. If this isn't fixed now, the world is heading to hell in a handbasket filled with zombie fruits and vegetables. We won't stand by and let farms like this one be destroyed."

Chapter 47

"IF THIS ISN'T FIXED now, the world is heading to hell in a handbasket filled with zombie fruits and vegetables."

Sarah snapped awake at the sound of the amplified voice from outside.

I fell asleep. Shit!

That surprised her, considering what she came here to do today. Was she too late? Did it already happen?

"We won't stand by and let farms like this one be destroyed."

It couldn't have happened yet, or the conference wouldn't still be going on.

She got out of the chair, stretched, and walked to the window. Outside, hundreds of people were gathered in the field, all staring straight ahead at the stage as whoever was up there had just switched to speaking Italian. Whatever he was saying, he sounded pretty angry.

She had once heard someone say, 'you're either arguing, or you're Italian,' in reference to how passionate these people were when speaking about anything. The Italians used hundreds of hand signals when talking, and Sarah knew almost none of them.

They sure add the word culture to agriculture, she thought as she stepped away from the view of the farmer's fields.

She placed an ear against the door.

Nothing. Not a sound.

She put the jacket on, got her gun ready, and lifted the small latch to unlock the door. She cracked it open and peeked out.

The dining room was empty. She opened the door wider and looked the full length of the dining and living room. Then she stepped up the stairs and checked to the left of the door. The entire area was empty. Even Betsy was nowhere to be seen.

With her gun leading the way, she put one foot in front of the other and headed for the bathroom. She prayed she wasn't too late. At any second, the sound of a high-powered rifle would signal that she had missed her chance. As long as she didn't hear that and the conference continued, there was still hope.

Just before the bathroom door, she checked over her shoulder.

Where's Betsy?

Police style, as if clearing a room, Sarah raised her gun to aim it at the ceiling, her back against the wall. She took two deep breaths and swung around into the bathroom, her weapon extended in front of her.

One man, dressed in black, sat on the closed toilet seat, his arms wrapped around the long shaft of a rifle, his eye on the sights. His black suit covered him from head to toe. Even his hands were covered in thin black gloves. She couldn't tell if it was De Luca or a hired hitman.

She visually swept the rest of the bathroom to ensure they were alone and then said, "Put it down."

The man barely flinched.

"I said put it down, or you win the prize behind door number one, which is a bullet in the back of the head."

The man maintained an eye on whatever he was looking at.

"Motherfucker," she said in frustration. "No more games. Drop the fucking weapon or die. That's it—"

His rifle spit a bullet. The crowd outside screamed in a horrific chorus.

Sarah blinked. Her gun faltered, her trigger finger sweaty. It slipped off the trigger guard, and the gun rotated in her hand so far she almost dropped it.

The man in black lifted off the floor as if he were propelled by springs. Light glinted off a long blade in his hand.

Sarah backed up one step, flipped the gun back into position, and pulled hard on the trigger guard. Her finger didn't get inside fast enough to shoot.

The man landed on her. She had to use her gun arm to block the knife. His weight forced her down until she hit the floor on her back, reigniting old wounds, her ribs aching.

He forced the knife hand down, the tip of the blade edging closer to her chest. She was losing the struggle of his strength against hers. She kicked her feet off the floor and brought them up to wrap around her opponent's waist. She locked her ankles and squeezed just as the tip of the knife tapped her chest. Then she reared back, pulling him partially off.

She screamed as she twisted, knocking the shooter sideways and into the hard stone floor of the bathroom.

He brought the knife around in a wide arc, aiming for Sarah's leg.

At the last second, she unlocked her ankles and moved her leg out of the way, hoping he would continue the arc to stab himself.

The knife flew out of his grip and across the room. He scrambled back and grabbed at something on the floor by his bag.

She brought the gun up in front of her. At the same time, he aimed a silenced weapon at her.

He fired before she had a chance.

Her gun was violently ripped from her hand, twisting two of her fingers back.

She screamed as the shooter clicked something on his weapon and took careful aim again. She was too far away to kick at him or scramble to cover. She was out of options.

"Say a prayer," he said. "It's goodnight time."

As his finger twitched, a blur bolted in from the bathroom door.

Betsy was airborne, her mouth wide. When her teeth came together, the shooter's arm was inside them, the gun all but forgotten as he struggled against the jaws clamped on him.

He squirmed under Betsy's weight as she bit and chewed to protect the new member of her pack.

Sarah scrambled to her gun, but the bullet that knocked it from her hand had rendered it useless.

Betsy was still fighting the shooter, but he was edging toward his bag again.

"Oh, no, you don't," Sarah said as she got to her feet.

Another knife came out of the side of the black bag by the toilet. The shooter grunted as blood covered his midsection now, his arm mangled. He raised the knife as Sarah got to him and kicked.

She connected perfectly, knocking the knife into the bathtub behind him.

With a perfect roundhouse kick, one Aaron would be proud of, her heel connected with the shooter's face.

His head snapped back, his eyes shut, and the back of his head bumped into the bathtub.

Betsy backed off the unconscious man. She sat beside him, blood dripping from her snout, pink tongue hanging out the side.

"Thanks, girl," Sarah whispered. "You saved my life."

Sarah pulled the black balaclava off the shooter's head, expecting to see Frank De Luca, but it wasn't him.

"Who the fuck are you?"

She had hoped it would all end here with Frank De Luca being arrested.

After tapping the top of Betsy's head, she couldn't ignore the pandemonium coming from outside.

She moved the sniper's rifle aside at the bathroom window and looked out.

***

Parkman ducked instinctively at the shot, as did everyone around him. The crowd went wild, running in all directions. Some people were running across a neighboring cornfield, others were headed toward the Tiber River.

The men on stage dove in front of the ministers like they were the president of the United States. A group of at least six men circled each minister and rushed them all off the stage and into waiting vehicles.

The crowd thinned as people ran.

Parkman examined the trees in the distance, the cars by the stage, and the train tracks behind the house.

Where could a sniper hide?

Then he looked up at the house.

No way. Where's the farmer?

Wouldn't the police have secured that?

He turned back to the stage to see what Delarusso was doing. Through binoculars, he scanned something near the farmer's house.

Parkman swiveled his gaze back to the house. There was movement in the window on the second floor.

He squinted and looked closer.

Fiery red hair billowed in the soft breeze as Sarah stuck her head out.

Delarusso shouted something in Italian from the stage. Parkman knew enough Italian to know it wasn't good for Sarah.

Shots fired. Tiny billows of rock dust burst around the second-floor window as the Italian authorities fired shot after shot where Sarah's head had just been.

"Cease fire," Parkman yelled.

Then he ran for the house.

***

People ran, the crowd below the window dispersing.

The cop from her hospital room shouted something from the podium, and dozens of officers looked her way, pulled their weapons, and fired.

She ducked back into the house.

"Holy shit! You have got to be kidding." She ran out the bathroom door. "Come on, Betsy."

She ran through the dining room, into the kitchen, and down the stairs, she had come up hours before.

How can they assume it was me? The shooter's unconscious in the bathroom.

She was about to jump through the door when it ripped open. She jumped back just in time.

"I'll shoot," Sarah yelled.

"Please don't," a familiar voice said. Darwin stuck his head in. "Come on. Follow me, quick."

She didn't need any more coaxing.

They ran through the bushes where she had hidden the Brit's mountain bike, ran across a dirt road, and onto the train tracks.

"Where are we going?" Sarah asked.

"This way."

"I know that. But where?"

"Just keep up," he shouted back.

The sounds of men shouting at the house for her to come out drifted through the trees. She ran harder, hoping Darwin knew the train schedule. To be killed by a regional train now after what had just happened would be shit luck.

The tracks curved, losing them to sight if someone were to check the tracks. They crossed a small bridge. A dilapidated building came up on the left. Darwin jumped from the tracks and ran for the building. Sarah followed, staying close.

His Fiat sat in front.

They jumped in, and he turned onto the road, gunning the small engine to get up to speed.

"How did you know?" Sarah asked, trying to catch her breath.

"I have someone who wants to meet you."

"Who?"

"I don't know."

"Darwin, what's going on?" Sarah asked.

"How come *you* don't know?" he asked, turning to look at her. "If you didn't write the note, then who did?"

"What note?"

The lines on his forehead thickened as he frowned. "Rosina found a note in the guest room where you stayed. You had to have been the one who wrote it."

Sarah thought about it for a moment. "Remember how I told you my sister works through me?"

He nodded.

"She must've written the note and left it for you. Maybe when I was sleeping because this is the first I've heard of it."

He said as he rolled his window up. "It told me what to do at the hospital and to be here to pick you up. It said you'd be running out of that house. I'm to deliver you to someone who wants to talk to you and then leave. My job is done after this, the note said."

"You're kidding, right?" Sarah asked.

He shook his head. "We're supposed to be in lockdown until tomorrow, but you can thank Rosina. She's the one who convinced me to do this after we saw the reports that Marconi was confirmed dead. The more mafia you eliminate, the safer our lives will be. So I made an exception."

"Well, for what it's worth, thanks."

He nodded and kept his eyes on the road. "This is it, though. I drop you off, and I'm out as far as the note said, anyway. I'd love to help more, but I have a family to think about now."

"Fair enough. You're out. Where are you dropping me off?"

"At a bed and breakfast on the E45 highway. According to the note, a man is there and wants to speak with you."

A man? Frank De Luca?

"Do you have anything else on this man?"

"He goes by, The Cowboy."

Chapter 48

SARAH THANKED DARWIN PROFUSELY as he pulled away. Once his Fiat was out of sight, headed toward Umbertide, she faced the front of the B&B.

A gorgeous building was built in what appeared to be a perfect square. A fenced-in garden sat to the right, on the sunny side. She assumed they pulled many of their meals from that garden.

Each window on the second floor had two circular flower pot holders at its base, with colorful flowers blossoming in the early spring. The front door was a dark wood engraved with a spectacular design unfamiliar to her.

Someone had done a lot of work to make this bed and breakfast stand out in its Italian heritage. Love and care were in every intricate detail.

Maybe one day she would own something she could take pride in other than a reliable gun.

She opened the small wire gate by the walkway and closed it behind her.

The feeling of being watched covered her like a soft blanket as she started for the front door. The door opened a crack, then opened wider.

An old woman stood in the doorway, her lips a straight line. The Italian sun over the years had played havoc on her features.

"Buonasera," the woman said in a gruff voice.

Sarah nodded, not knowing what to say in Italian. "The Cowboy?"

The woman stepped back from the door, picked up a laundry basket, and walked away.

"Humph," Sarah mumbled to herself.

She stepped inside the front door. A younger woman was in the hall near the back, wearing a floral summer dress and a large smile.

"Hello, you American?" the woman asked as she entered the front foyer.

"Ahh, English," Sarah said. "Yes, I'm here to meet a friend."

"We only have one guest at the moment. I'll go ring him. You can wait in the games room."

The woman gestured to her left. Sarah headed that way.

The games room was impressive. She took in the pool table, the soft couch, and the boxed games on the table beside the couch. A dart board took up the far corner. The area to stand while throwing the darts was distanced out with markers on the carpeted floor. A foosball table was situated along the wall by the window.

Sarah sat on the couch to allow a clear view of the door.

She arranged her jacket so that the butt of Darwin's gun would be easy to grab if the man who entered the games room was Frank De Luca. Even though Darwin's gun was useless now, it still posed enough threat to aim it at someone.

She suspected Frank De Luca had been monitoring the GMO conference and the performance of his hitman and that he wouldn't be relaxing in his room at a B&B along the highway.

Heavy footfalls came down the stairs.

A moment later, a man wearing cowboy boots and a brown cowboy hat stepped inside the door to the games room. He looked vaguely familiar, the man she had glimpsed as she chased him down the escalator at the train station in Rome.

He was also very good-looking in a rugged sense. Normally the cowboy fashion looked stupid to her unless she was at a rodeo, which she had never been to, but with him, it added to his looks.

He tipped his hat. "Good afternoon, ma'am." If he was surprised she was here, he didn't show it.

"Don't," she said.

He cocked his head to the side and tightened his facial muscles. As his teeth clenched, a bulge formed at the back of his jaw.

"Ma'am?"

"Don't call me ma'am. I'm not one of those."

His face relaxed in understanding. "I apologize. How did you know I was staying here? How did you find me?"

"My sister told a friend …" She shook her head. "Don't worry about it. Long story." She got off the couch.

"What happened at the conference?" he asked. "Were

you there?"

She told him how a shooter had attempted to kill someone. Everyone ran from the area. She left Darwin out of the story.

"Wish I was there," he said, still standing in the doorway.

"Where are you from?"

"Calgary, Alberta. Heard of it?"

"Seriously?"

"May I?" He gestured for the other end of the couch.

She nodded.

He sat down, straightened his jeans, extended his long legs, and crossed them at the ankles.

She sat back down, too.

"I've met a lot of Americans who don't know Canadian geography that well. It's okay, though. I was only asking if you had heard of it because that's what I do. I ask questions."

"What is it you do, exactly?"

"I ask questions," he repeated.

She nodded and looked away.

Where the hell is this going?

"Why did you come to Italy?" he asked.

"You first. What's your story? Why are you so far from home?"

"Coffee first." He got up and strode from the room.

What a character.

A few minutes later, he returned with two cups of coffee and a small tray of biscotti.

"You okay with espresso?" he asked.

"Yes."

They sipped in silence and ate the biscotti.

"Why did you run from me in Rome?" Sarah asked.

"Because your hotel room was being watched. I decided we couldn't talk until you were on the move. Then your partner was shot. I just had to leave the area."

Sarah finished her espresso and set the empty cup down. "I came to Italy to gather information on Sam "The Dealer" Marconi, but he's dead now, and I'm looking for a man named Frank De Luca."

The Cowboy started at the mention of Frank's name.

"You know this man?" Sarah asked.

"Who doesn't? De Luca's a legend. No one ever gets close to him."

"I did."

The Cowboy's eyes widened.

She explained what had happened the day De Luca tried to tell her that he was The Cowboy and how she had smelled a rat. De Luca was the one who blew up the restaurant in Umbertide's piazza, and he was the one who hired a hitman to kill the two ministers at the conference an hour ago.

They sat for a moment in silence.

"Your turn," Sarah said. "Tell me about you. Gain my trust."

The Cowboy twisted in his seat to face her better.

"Being an investigative reporter is a thankless endeavor. It makes my editor impatient and angers powerful people."

"I can only imagine."

"After getting my bachelor's in journalism, I wanted to go deep, learn about something corrupt, and even become a whistleblower myself. So I asked tough questions and wouldn't leave an issue alone until I was satisfied I had done all I could."

Sarah leaned back, giving him her undivided attention.

"I was advised against this job, but my passion for truth and justice thrust me forward. That and having a father as a criminal judge taught me a thing or two about justice. This is a risky business. I thought a story on GMOs would be safe enough, but I was wrong. I've received death threats, been followed, and even had a car attempt to run me over."

"Wow."

"I've discovered that the company wanting their GMOs grown in Italy has millions of dollars funneling into certain political campaigns here. I've followed the money trail as best I could and learned that the minister of—"

"Finance," Sarah finished for him. "Silvio Capelli."

"Right. How did you know?"

"De Luca told me."

"I'm confused. If Capelli is bought and paid for, and he hired Marconi or De Luca, why would he tell someone like you information like that?"

"I suspect Capelli has done something to piss De Luca off. Anyone else of interest on this money trail?"

"The trail led to one more name." The Cowboy paused to adjust his hat, pushing his hair up under it. "The senior officer of the state police in Umbertide, Antonio Delarusso."

Sarah snapped her fingers. "That's why he's being such an asshole." She met The Cowboy's eyes. "He wanted me cuffed, taken to an airplane, and flown out of Italy. He said he would tell his men to shoot me on sight if I didn't leave Italy immediately. He wouldn't listen to reason when I tried to explain what happened the night of the explosion." She looked away in a daze. "I should've picked up on it sooner."

"Don't beat yourself up. Once there's enough money involved, people go to great lengths to silence others. An old colleague of mine, Don, once did a piece called the 'Nuclear Family.' It was about the leaks from nuclear power stations across America and how one day, the radiation will cause birth defects and deformities in our future children. He focused on a plant where he had an insider feeding him raw data. Don is dead now, and his principal informant is still incarcerated." He paused.

Sarah soaked up every word. These people were just like her; only their weapon was ink.

"I lost my job because I refused to relent," he continued. "I can't contact my family until this is over. I'm running out of money and always have to look over my shoulder. The only casualty of all this terror and fear is the truth, justice. So far, you're the only one going after it, too. You're the only one still alive I hope I can trust."

Sarah rested her head on her hands for a moment. "As far as the world knows, I'm dead right now. My parents are even preparing for my funeral, and I can't do anything about that until this is over. I guess we both have it bad." She crossed her arms and draped a leg over the other. "Tell me more about GMOs. Why are they so important that people will kill for them?"

"Global domination of the food supply," he said. "I'll get into that in a minute. But first, I have to explain why I wanted to see you in the first place."

"I'm listening."

"There's a way to bring them all together. I have an idea. If this works, you expose Delarusso and Capelli and nab De Luca in the process."

"You're kidding, right?"

"No, but it would involve you being shot. I would

threaten to expose them to the international community through the press if they didn't give you medical aid—no questions asked."

Sarah smiled. "I'm liking where this is going."

Chapter 49

PARKMAN HAD BEEN ORDERED out of the way. No one had seen Sarah leave. It took them all of fifteen minutes to clear the house after having a difficult time with a German shepherd.

"Someone find the farmer who owns this place," Delarusso yelled. Parkman picked up most of the Italian. Delarusso continued, "I thought this building was already cleared. Who's responsible for this?"

An officer dressed in black fatigues stepped forward. "I was, sir."

"Report back to base. Clear the area."

The officer walked away, a pensive look on his face.

When Parkman turned back to Delarusso, he was watching him.

"What are you doing here?" Delarusso asked.

"Same thing you are," Parkman shouted back.

"I don't think so. Arrest this man."

Officers moved in.

"What are you doing?" Parkman asked.

"Getting a tighter grip on this case. You aren't going anywhere until we find that red-haired girl of yours. Then I will personally escort you to the airport because your girl will stay behind in our jail if she makes it."

"You had better hope she makes it."

Delarusso glared at Parkman. After a heartbeat, he closed the distance between them to stand nose to nose.

"Is that a threat?"

"Sarah Roberts is an American citizen who is only in Italy because she was asked to be here by the Italian authorities. If for any reason, you are not aiding in her investigation, then you are hindering it. If anything happens to her, you will be questioned. Back in the States, we call that an investigation, which means we would examine intent and motive. For example, why wouldn't you help a small red-haired girl in her twenties who is working for your country? What's in it for you to not help? How do you—"

"Get him out of my sight," Delarusso shouted at the officers on either side of Parkman.

Along the way to the small Italian police cars, Parkman saw Kierian being forced into the back seat of another car.

Sorry, Sarah. You're on your own.

Chapter 50

SARAH AND THE COWBOY went outside to the pergola in the back. The old woman had just finished hanging up bed sheets to dry. She collected her basket and headed back inside.

The flat fields extended for miles until the mountains rose in the distance.

"Italy's gorgeous," Sarah said. "I just wish I could enjoy it more."

"Once this is all over, maybe you could."

She sat in a lounge chair and brought her knees up to her chest, still wearing Darwin's jacket like a safety blanket.

"Tell me about GMOs. Why are you so against them? Let me play devil's advocate here."

"Sure, but first, I'll ask them to bring more coffee. An Americano this time."

"Perfect."

She waited by herself, breathing in the fresh air, relaxing, gathering her thoughts, and mentally preparing for what she still had to do. Her mind wandered to Aaron, her parents. What were they going through at that moment?

"We're all set for coffee." The Cowboy took a seat across a small circular table between them. "About GMOs … Henry Kissinger once said, 'who controls the food supply, controls the people …'"

"But how could GMOs lead to controlling the food supply?" Sarah asked. "You can't own Mother Nature."

"Exactly, but you can patent your own design. Once companies like Monsanto designed a seed that led to a pesticide-producing crop, it became patentable. They made the seed. They own it. They can patent it."

"Pesticide-producing crop?"

"That's a crop that produces its own toxic insecticide. When an insect bites it, the toxin attacks the insect's nervous system and kills them."

"And humans eat this crop? With the toxin still in it?"

He nodded. "Humans, pigs, cows …"

"What? How? I thought cows ate grass."

"They used to. Now many of them are corn and soy fed. Pigs fed with GMO corn had an almost three hundred percent increase in severe stomach inflammation compared to those fed non-GMO diets."

"Why hasn't this been stopped, then?"

"Big business. Lots of money involved."

The door opened behind them. The younger woman stepped out onto the back deck with a tray in hand.

"Here's a couple of coffees. I brought bread with mortadella."

"Grazie," Cowboy said.

The woman set the tray down and headed toward the garden.

"What's mortadella?" Sarah asked when their host was far enough away.

"It's really just a large Italian sausage made of heat-cured pork. Similar to bologna in America, but tastier."

"Is this safe to eat after what you just told me about pigs?"

"It is here. This B&B is completely organic. That's why I'm here."

Sarah ripped off a piece of the bread and laid the mortadella on top. After biting in, she washed it down with the hot coffee.

"Holy shit."

"I know. Good, eh?"

"We have to discuss your plan to get them out into the open," Sarah said between bites.

"We will, but first, a couple more things about GMOs."

"Go ahead."

"A growing amount of data has connected GMOs with health problems and environmental damage. Experiments have *proven* that eating GMOs can cause cancerous tumors, infertility, and birth defects."

"Sounds like radiation poisoning."

"Funny you should say that. The same company that created nerve gas and Agent Orange, which is still affecting babies born in Vietnam today, brings you pesticides, insecticides, and GMO food. Pesticide is just another word for a modified version of nerve gas."

She stopped chewing and stared at him. "How come I don't know this? How come the general public isn't aware?

Why hasn't the FDA protected us?"

He winced. "I hate those three letters. The FDA is bought and paid for already. But over here in Europe, countries are fighting back. Did you see what they did in Hungary?"

Sarah shook her head.

"They torched five-hundred hectares of genetically modified corn to eradicate GMOs from their food supply. GMOs are banned now in over thirty countries worldwide, and labeling is required in over fifty."

"Torched? As in fire?"

"Yes." He nodded. "To avoid cross-pollination. Fire destroys the DNA and breaks down vegetable matter into carbon and mineral ash. Cornfields that were once dangerous are now rendered harmless. The intense heat destroys the engineered DNA created in a lab by people who think they can outsmart Mother Nature. Even France has a ban on Frankencorn."

"This is serious. How come I don't know any of it? I understood that eating healthy meant organic, but not all the reasons. I feel sick now."

She set her coffee down and stretched her legs, the sun warming her skin.

"Here's how it breaks down," he said as he leaned forward and held the other hand's index finger. "Almost all the soy, corn, and canola oil in the world is GMO now." He pulled one finger down. "Practically every processed food found in grocery stores contains some form of corn, like high-fructose corn syrup, soy, cottonseed or canola." He lowered another finger. "Crackers, cookies, cereals, and snack foods are all considered non-human food because of all the chemicals in them." He lowered another finger. "For example, blueberry muffin mix doesn't actually have any blueberries in it. It's a chemical additive created in a lab to look and taste like blueberries, colored with two different blue dyes." He lowered his last finger. "Whatever contains artificial sweetener contains GMOs, too."

"So what can people safely eat? What's human food?"

"Anything in a recognized organic store, cows and other animals that aren't fed GMO corn or soy—basically cows that are grass-fed, and people should plant their own gardens. The rule of thumb is if it's processed food, it's not human food. Hundreds of years ago, nothing was processed. Even our wheat has been compromised."

"Okay, too much in one sitting," Sarah said as she set the bread back on the tray.

"Italy's proposed ban on GMOs came in with eighty percent public support. That's why today's conference was so important."

"Doesn't the European Union govern that sort of thing?" Sarah asked.

"The European Food and Safety Authority is Europe's FDA. Individual governments are able to introduce safeguards if they feel the food supply is threatened or there are environmental risks."

"Anything else I should know before we expose these assholes?"

He smiled and adjusted himself in his seat. "We're winning. Slowly, but globally, we're winning."

"How?"

"There was a March Against Monsanto which happened last May where two million people participated in solidarity protests around the globe to raise public awareness of

Monsanto's toxic legacy. The next one is taking place this coming October twelfth, when an expected four million people will attend. Since then, their stock prices have decreased as investors realize they're not a good long-term investment anymore. We're finally getting to them."

His eyes watered as he looked away, the shadow of his hat unable to hide his joy.

"What's your plan for tonight?" she asked. "Tell me the details."

He wiped his face, took a long sip from his coffee, and stood. He walked a few feet away and kept his back to her.

"I will write up everything I know and suspect to be true." He turned around. "I will name names and cover the money trail that leads to the minister of finance and the senior officer of the state police. Then I will connect them to Marconi and the sniper at the farmhouse today. Once that's done, I will add that you tried to stop it all and say that I shot you."

"But why would you shoot me? They think we're allies."

"In investigative journalism, nobody's my ally. Only my editor. But I will convince them that we fought. You wanted to hunt them down yourself, and I couldn't allow that. I wanted them to face justice. You tried to leave. We argued. I shot you. I will email this to Capelli, the finance minister, and Delarusso at the state police and tell them that I feel terrible. The guilt is tearing me up. They are to help you at the hospital and let you leave, or I expose the story."

"You do know that you're going to have every legal authority come down on you for this, right?"

He shrugged. "That's where you come in."

"How?"

"You're supposed to be shot. When they send De Luca or some other hitman, you deal with him, and we'll have all the evidence to nail these guys to the wall. You just have to be at the Umbertide hospital at midnight tonight."

"Why tonight? And can you write all that up that fast?"

"It's already written. That's what I've been doing here. My investigation is complete, and I chose tonight because all those men are still local."

"What about Frank De Luca?"

"He's the one we're trying to bring out of the woodwork. He's not a ghost; he's a cockroach. But you'll have the light switch in your hand, and when you flick it on, you will catch all these men trying to kill you. I have a friend who works at the hospital. He'll do me a favor. That's why I thought the hospital was your best location." He slapped his hands together and rubbed them back and forth. "Oh, this is going to be great."

"Glad you think so. You don't get shot."

Chapter 51

Sarah rode into Umbertide with the young woman who ran the B&B. The woman had a dozen questions about America but was mostly convinced the country was made of money. Whoever lived in the land of plenty had to be rich.

Sarah attempted to allay those assumptions but decided to leave the nice Italian woman with her visions of grandeur.

Three blocks short of Umbertide's hospital was a stunning residential area, where quaint two-story homes lined each side of the streets, tiny balconies on the second floor of each house. Flowers and gardens indigenous to the Italian lifestyle littered the windows, lawns, and gates of almost every home.

Sarah got out and walked the rest of the way as her driver turned around and headed back to the B&B south of the city.

The email had been sent in the late afternoon to the head of the state police for this area, Antonio Delarusso, and the

Minister of Finance, Silvio Capelli. It outlined everything The Cowboy had discovered regarding their involvement with the major GMO corporations. It detailed their plans as representatives of Italy to aid in that venture and how they had been paid handsomely in campaign money, contributions, and other donations in their name.

Finally, the emails said that Sarah Roberts needed medical care and would be immediately dropped off at the Umbertide hospital at midnight. She was to be given the best doctors, and the best care money could buy, then allowed safe passage to the United States. At that time, the information in the email would be destroyed. The reason The Cowboy gave was he didn't want to spend the rest of his life looking over his shoulder or in jail for attempted murder since he was the one who shot Sarah by accident. If Sarah were hurt in any way, he would have no choice but to follow through with his threats and make all the information he had public knowledge.

Sarah checked her watch, which miraculously still worked after all that she had been through.

11:05 p.m.

Almost an hour left to prepare.

An ambulance pulled along the street, driving slowly as if looking for an address. The driver was The Cowboy's friend and supposedly owed The Cowboy a favor. He had agreed to sneak an ambulance out and pick Sarah up.

She stepped out onto the road and caught his attention. The vehicle slowed. At the passenger door, the driver nodded at her.

"Sarah?" he asked.

She nodded back at him.

"Hop in," he said in accented English.

When she opened the door, the interior light turned on. She ducked low and slammed the door, killing the light.

"You wanna hop in the back?"

She climbed out of the front seat through a little door and into the rear.

"Lie down on the stretcher and pull the white blanket over your head. I'll drive us back to emerg."

She did as she was told. The ambulance started moving again. She closed her eyes and breathed steadily.

"How well do you know Ernesto?" the driver asked.

"Ernesto?"

"He didn't tell you his name?"

"No."

"Didn't think he would. Ever since people started calling him The Cowboy, he stopped giving his real name. He never liked Ernesto Eugene Everton. We met fifteen years ago on a story he was doing here in Umbria. He did the right thing by my family. Got me out of a tragic situation. Now I'm doing him a favor. Although I can't imagine why anyone would want to be smuggled *into* a hospital."

"It's better you don't know, but I can assure you, none of it will fall back on you."

"Ernesto explained that. I trust him. He could've used my name in the piece he wrote all those years ago, but he didn't. He protected me when I was only eight years old. Taught me a lesson on how to keep my word. Had he used my name, it would've ruined my life. Because of him, I got a good education and a good job. I'm eternally grateful."

"Is there a way you can admit me as a gunshot victim without it being traced back to you?"

"Yes."

"What room am I going to be in?"

"Room 202."

"Got it."

She gripped the sides of the stretcher so she wouldn't roll off and meditated on what she had to do. She had no specific plan, but waiting for De Luca inside the hospital was all she needed.

When they met again, Frank De Luca would be surprised.

They all will be.

Chapter 52

Frank De Luca had never yearned to kill a man as much as he wanted to kill his employer, Silvio Capelli. Usually, he remained detached, his kills impersonal, business. But with Capelli, his emotions had gotten involved, and now it was personal.

The kind of information in the email sent to Capelli by The Cowboy, who Frank had warned Capelli about in Rome, was lethal. If they didn't shut The Cowboy down and erase everything he had, everyone, including him, would have to disappear for a while. His movements would be seriously constrained in the coming years. His identity would have to be altered again, his ID redone. Running would be the new existence, at least in the short term.

In order to get to The Cowboy, Sarah couldn't be killed. Instead, Capelli had come up with the idea to make her tell him where The Cowboy was hiding, then kill her.

Frank De Luca didn't kidnap people or torture them for information. He simply killed them. That's what people like Capelli hired him for.

One of Frank's best snipers was arrested in the bathroom of the farmer's house because of Sarah. All De Luca saw when the name Sarah Roberts crossed his mind was blood on her decapitated face.

"You hired me to do a job," De Luca breathed into the phone. "As I said before, once we enter into a contract, I fulfill my end and expect you to fulfill yours. Your dealer has left the game, but I don't see my compensation."

"Because I added a clause. At midnight, when our friend is mended at the hospital, bring her to me. I will compensate you for what I owe you and reward you handsomely for the delivery."

"That wasn't our agreement. But if you're willing to enter into a new one, how much are we discussing?"

"One million euros."

"Two."

"Done. Just be there by one in the morning."

"What assurances do I have?"

"Assurances?"

"How do I know I'm not walking into an ambush? You and your pal Delarusso could have every cop in Italy surrounding that hospital. Convince me this isn't a trap."

"I thought you were smart." There was an intake of breath on the other end of the line. "I forwarded part of the email to your phone. You saw it with your own eyes. If you and Sarah are captured or killed, that doesn't solve The Cowboy problem, does it? I need Sarah here. Then you get that Cowboy any way you see fit. At no time will I attempt to stop you. It serves no purpose for me."

"You tried once with The Dealer."

"So naturally, you'd think I'd try again?"

"Naturally."

"Just bring that girl."

Frank clicked off the line. He scanned the hospital's second-floor windows. It was more than a half hour before Sarah would arrive. He needed to be inside and ready, which meant he couldn't be out here watching for the police.

Capelli, you had better not fuck with me.

Soon the world could go on believing Sarah was dead. Then he would wait for the transfer of all the funds. He might even wait a week or two and let Silvio Capelli feel he was safe, untouchable. Allow him to believe that working with The Ghost was a mistake, but glad it was over.

Then he would come out of the shadows one night, and Capelli would feel a soft punch in the back of the head.

Frank smiled as he walked toward the main doors at the front of the hospital.

An ambulance drove by, the lights off. He slowed his pace and watched as the driver angled the vehicle to the side of the building.

Sarah?

Frank stopped and leaned against a tree. The ambulance driver got out and walked around to the back door. Another paramedic emerged from the hospital and helped to pull a stretcher out of the back of the ambulance.

A body was on the stretcher, the entire length covered in a white blanket.

A stiff being delivered to the morgue.

Frank entered the hospital, wondering how many more

stiffs would visit the morgue that night.

Sarah Roberts, for sure. How could one girl piss off so many people?

There was no way he would kidnap Sarah for Capelli. He didn't work for Capelli anymore. Sarah dies, then he takes her body to Capelli.

Let's see what he thinks about our arrangement then.

Or maybe he would just take her head.

He smiled for the second time that night.

Yeah, that's what I'll do.

Chapter 53

Sarah waited until the ambulance driver told her it was safe to get up.

She jumped from the stretcher and landed on both feet.

"Room 202?"

He pointed along the corridor. "At the end, take the elevator to the second floor. Your room is beside the stairwell, as requested by our mutual friend."

"Grazie."

She took the stairs instead of the elevator. Once on the second floor, she went door to door searching for a linen closet of some kind.

Four doors down from room 202, she entered the janitor's room and almost tripped over the bucket and mop sitting just inside the door.

Once the door was shut, she secured it from the inside and moved back to the far wall to wait. Only twenty minutes left until showtime.

The only setback would be if De Luca sent another hired gun in his place, but Sarah didn't think he would. Getting to her had become personal for him. Almost killing her in the explosion wouldn't be enough. He would want to be the one to do it now so he could guarantee it was done right.

He had a name to live up to. He was The Ghost, and Sarah had seen his face. That was enough to make sure he was here tonight.

She could handle him. She only hoped The Cowboy did his part and rallied Interpol to swoop in and pick up Delarusso and Capelli simultaneously just after midnight.

The evidence was too hard to ignore. These men had to answer for what they had done and the lives they had ruined.

Knowing those men were taken care of, Sarah could focus on ensuring Frank De Luca answered for what he had done.

She would have it no other way.

Chapter 54

FRANK WANDERED AROUND THE hospital's main entrance, learning its hallways and exit points, and then waited on a bench outside, holding a newspaper in front of his face.

At midnight, the hospital remained quiet. He waited until five minutes after. No ambulance movement, and no one was being rushed to emergency as far as he could tell.

Did Sarah set me up?

It was a small hospital in a city of 17,000. They were on midnight staff at this late hour, and most patients were asleep.

The hospital and surrounding area remained quiet. No cops.

Frank waited a few more minutes, keeping a sharp eye on the grounds. He neatly folded the newspaper, set it down on the bench, and strode inside the hospital.

The clock on the wall said it was eight minutes past midnight. At the admittance desk, he smiled at the woman.

"Can I help you?" she asked in Italian.

"I'm looking for a friend who was admitted earlier."

"Visiting hours are over."

Inside, he chastised himself for not thinking this through better. Outside, he appeared calm and understanding.

"Of course." He offered her a smile. "This friend is more of a girlfriend. She was hurt this evening. Sarah Roberts. Could you look her name up and at least reassure me she's in your system?"

The woman turned to her computer and typed, then used her mouse.

"Yes, we have her here." The woman turned back to him. "But you'll have to come back tomorrow."

"Of course," he said.

He adjusted his jacket and walked outside. Once out of her sight, he headed along the side of the building around toward the emergency doors. A quick check of the area, the parking lot, and the streets reassured him his allies weren't liars. He detected no police presence.

He changed his tactics once inside emerg. One of the ambulance attendants he'd seen earlier was eating a sandwich while typing into his phone.

"Can you help me?" he asked in a panic.

"Sure," the guy said, his mouth half full.

"Where would they put a gunshot victim? What floor?"

"That depends. They would be brought in and probably head straight to surgery. That's all on the second floor. Depending on the outcome, they could go to recover on the third or fourth floor, but they may end up in ICU for a while."

"Thanks, you're a pal."

Frank hurried for the stairwell.

When he hit the door, he glanced back and saw the ambulance driver eating again, staring down at his phone.

On the second floor, Frank entered the first room. An old man slept in the near dark, a small light on the end table lit up the corner by the window. In a cast, the man's leg was suspended from chains in the ceiling.

Frank opened the closet doors quietly and found a hospital gown. He slipped it on over his clothes and tied it so tight that most of his clothes weren't visible.

His pants could be seen under the gown, but he wanted to hide from patients, not hospital personnel.

He pulled out his gun and placed it against his leg, then slipped out of the room.

A lone woman sat behind a counter in the middle of the hall. The late-shift nurse. He was so close to Sarah that he could almost feel it.

As he approached, the nurse looked up. "What are you up so late for? What room are you in?"

"Couldn't sleep," he said.

He walked around the counter without losing a step and entered from the back.

"Hey, you can't come back here—"

She pulled away from him, but he grabbed her arm and pulled her close.

"Where's the morphine?"

She grunted under his grip, trying to fight him and dislodge his hand.

He dropped his forehead, which connected with the bridge of her nose. She tried to cry out, but he covered her mouth to eclipse any sound. Her eyes watered, and she groaned as blood seeped from her nostrils.

He released her mouth so she could breathe and then asked again, "Where's the morphine?"

She wiped blood off her mouth and held her nose with both hands.

"You broke my nose," she said in a nasal voice.

"Morphine?"

She pointed toward the room behind the desk area.

"Show me."

He grabbed her arm and dragged her toward the room.

"Fill two syringes with enough morphine to knock someone out," he said. "Do it fast, or you'll need some yourself."

He aimed the weapon at her chest.

Shaking, the woman used a key to open a cabinet and ripped the packaging off two needles. After filling both needles to the top, she held them out for him.

He took one needle and nodded at her, "Stick yourself in the thigh."

Her eyes widened as she looked at the needle.

He brought his arm up and looked at his watch. "I'll give you three seconds to do it, or I'll shoot you."

Blood dripped off her chin, landing in tiny splats on the hospital floor in front of her shoes. She looked down at it, then back at him.

"One ..."

She got down slowly and placed her butt on the floor.

"Two ..."

She rolled her white uniform up to expose her thigh and brought the needle to the edge of her skin.

"Three ..."

She pushed the needle in and plunged the morphine into her bloodstream. Then she laid her head back and waited.

He moved backward, the gun still aimed at her, and shut the door to the back room. He lowered the weapon out of sight in case someone new was in the corridor and watched her through the glass window. After half a minute, she remained motionless.

It was already fifteen minutes after twelve. Sarah Roberts was likely on this floor. According to the email, she had a bullet wound.

So how come there wasn't any noise? No doctors in surgery scrubs, no one coming or going?

Something about this was wrong on so many levels.

The urge to leave the hospital and go after her at a later date struck him. Was he getting sloppy because of his emotions?

He wondered if Sarah could be that good to have both Delarusso's and Capelli's emails and set it up so that he would be forced to come here.

No, he didn't think so. She was a child playing in an adult's world. She was here. She was in the hospital. The police weren't coming. Delarusso wouldn't risk pissing him off.

Frank left the nurses' station to look for Sarah with the gun in one hand and the syringe in the other.

Chapter 55

SARAH PLACED THE JANITOR'S coat around her shoulders. The jacket was too big, but it wrapped her up well enough to cover her clothes. She transferred the gun into the coat pocket, pulled her hair into a tight bun, and placed a cap on her head to hold the hair in.

Then she wet her hands and applied a touch of dirt to each cheek. Once she was ready, she added water to the bucket.

It was just after midnight. Whoever was coming for her would be here already.

She opened the door, turned around, and walked out backward, pulling the mop and bucket with her. She dipped the mop in the water, twisted it, and wrung it out.

When the mop hit the floor, she nonchalantly gazed toward room 202. The nurses' station was behind her. Someone was walking her way, their shoes not clanking down but squeezing softly on the waxed floor.

Frank?

The shoes drew closer. She estimated ten feet in distance. Then six. Then five.

If the person were hospital personnel, she would apologize for her response and explain that she was startled.

The shoes slowed behind her.

She gripped the mop's wooden handle tight. Then she dropped and spun, swinging the mop in a wide arc, aiming for the feet of the person behind her.

A gun fired, and the report was extremely loud.

The mop connected with Frank's left shin. He bent over but didn't fall.

Her body surged into panic mode. She spun the mop handle up and swiped at his gun before he could right himself and try to shoot again. The tip of the mop connected with the barrel of the weapon solidly, knocking it from Frank's grip. The gun already forgotten, he lunged at her with his other hand. She didn't have time to examine what was in that hand as she let go of the mop and thrust upward, her fist heading for his groin. He sidestepped, and she missed.

A sharp bee sting hit her side.

They were too close. She was still low to the ground, Frank standing above her. She needed to move away to collect herself.

She tried to dive away, but there was resistance on her side where she had felt the sharp pain.

Frank grunted and slipped on the wet floor where she had just mopped.

Both of them hit the floor four feet from each other. Their eyes met. Sarah looked down at her side without wasting time to see what had stung her.

A needle.

"What did you—"

She yanked the needle out, a tiny squirt of blood coming with it. The needle had been plunged about a quarter of the way.

When she looked up, he had retrieved his gun.

They both heard the sirens at the same time.

"Hey," someone from down the hallway said.

Another door opened as patients woke up.

A door opened at the end of the corridor. Frank fired his weapon that way. The door slammed shut.

Sarah frantically reached into the janitor's pocket and grabbed her gun, but her body felt weak, liquid.

"Don't," Frank said.

Darwin's gun was broken. Pulling out a useless gun was risky, but she had no other play.

The sirens were close.

"Get up," Frank said.

She let go of the gun, her vision blurring.

He grabbed her arm and yanked her to her feet.

"You just got a small extension on life. You're going to help me get out of here."

She felt woozy, but she had to fight him. Her attempt to struggle was futile.

The sirens were so loud she thought police cars had entered the second floor.

Her eyes got heavy.

How could I let this happen?

She had a plan. They had a plan. The authorities were supposed to wait until just after midnight to pick up

Delarusso and Capelli. Sarah was to handle The Ghost.

She had a mop, a bucket, and a will to fight. He was a professional. But so was she. It was supposed to work.

But now she was being dragged downstairs. Someone yelled. A gun went off somewhere.

She barely winced at the sound. Whatever he had pricked her with coursed through her bloodstream.

I'm so sorry, Aaron ...

Chapter 56

FRANK COULDN'T BELIEVE DELARUSSO or Capelli would risk the police coming down on him. The nurse was out cold, possibly dying from an overdose. The gunfire would have woken up people, but the police response was too swift to be because of that.

Someone had double-crossed him. He suspected he'd be shot if he walked out of the hospital alone. Walking out with Sarah was no guarantee of safety, but it was all he had.

At the bottom of the stairs, as he pulled Sarah along the corridor toward the exit, officers ran in through the far doors, guns drawn.

He fired at them. They didn't return fire. He held a hospital employee in his arms. Sarah in the janitor's jacket gave him an edge.

He turned toward the emergency doors.

Someone shouted commands from outside.

The same paramedic who had been eating a sandwich earlier stood outside watching all the police cars and officers form a perimeter around the building. Frank yanked Sarah along with him until he was behind the paramedic.

Startled, the kid spun around and jumped back.

"Open the ambulance's back door," Frank ordered, waving his gun impatiently.

The kid rushed to do as he was told.

"Get in the front and drive this thing out of here," he said as he dropped Sarah onto the back bumper. He picked her legs up and tossed them in. She curled into a ball and lay still.

He held the weapon on the kid until he sat in the front seat and closed the door. Then Frank jumped in the back and closed both doors behind him.

"Drive!" he yelled.

The kid slumped in his seat and drove.

"What happened to her?" the kid asked.

"Shut up and drive. Faster!"

The kid dropped the accelerator, nearly knocking Frank off his feet. He stepped over Sarah's inert form and moved toward the front.

The men surrounding the hospital aimed their weapons at the escaping vehicle, but no one fired. They couldn't shoot an ambulance with an innocent paramedic driving, even if it held the man they wanted.

Through the back window, he saw officers running for their vehicles.

This wouldn't work long-term. He had to think of something else.

He looked back at Sarah. There was no leg wound like

Capelli's email had said. It had been a trap. Sarah had baited him.

But now the tables had turned. She was a child playing around in the big world. That would cost her.

She moved on the floor, not completely out yet.

"Where am I going?" the kid asked.

"Out of Umbertide. Go for the highway. Put on the sirens. Drive faster. Don't stop for anything, or I will turn your brains to mush." He thrust the gun in front of the kid's face.

"O-O-kay," the kid stuttered.

Frank smelled urine. The kid had pissed himself.

Good. He better be scared.

When he turned around, Sarah was on her feet, a feral expression on her face. Behind her, through the back windows, the police cars were out of sight.

They were alone, already turning onto the E45.

He smiled at Sarah and brought his weapon around toward her.

Then the driver slammed on the brakes.

Chapter 57

THE FOGGINESS MADE HER want to sleep. Comfort came with curling up. Whatever it was, Frank had injected felt so good.

Frank De Luca.

Her mind screamed his name.

Aaron.

This name shouted through her consciousness.

Her right hand numbed, then jerked. Her leg jerked.

Not now, Vivian. Sleepy time.

Her body jerked so hard again that her ribs ached. Someone yelled for the driver to go faster. The vehicle lurched forward. She curled into the fetal position and waited for sleep.

But her body jerked again.

What?

The ground moved under her. She slid sideways and smacked the wall. Then the driver took another corner too fast. She wanted to yell at him to slow down.

A man said something about going even faster.

She fought to open her eyes.

Her body spasmed. Her limbs seized, became rigid, relaxed, then seized again.

Let me go. I'm too tired.

Her legs kicked out, banged something, then a full-body seizure struck. Her adrenaline spiked. The vehicle was on a long corner of some kind, like a highway ramp. She was jammed into a corner and couldn't move.

At the end of the ramp, she rolled into the center of the floor, and the seizure ended.

She opened her eyes. An ambulance.

Frank De Luca.

With great effort, she rolled over and got to her knees. Wavering for a moment, she smacked her ribs where they had broken the month before.

A dull pain shot through them. It was like she had taken twenty Advil. Yesterday she would have shouted, but today the pain was enough to get her to her feet.

Frank turned around. Their eyes met.

He smiled and aimed his gun at her.

Then the driver slammed on the brakes, and Sarah shot forward. She hit Frank so hard with all her 135 pounds of trim, muscled weight, they propelled between the front seats and into the dash, Frank's back taking most of the impact.

Sarah was energized, on fire. Nothing seemed to hurt, but at the same time, she felt weak and on the verge of sleep.

They wrestled, grappling for the gun. The vehicle came to a complete stop, and the driver jumped out, the interior light flickering on, the driver's side door wide open.

Her weakness lost the battle.

Frank rolled her off him, favoring an injured back.

"Help," the driver yelled. It sounded like he was talking to someone. Another car door slammed nearby.

Get in here and help me.

She had landed upside down in the passenger seat, her shoulder blades on the floor mat, feet against the backrest of the seat. In her awkward position and with muscle fatigue, she was paralyzed.

Frank managed to pull himself up into the driver's seat, wincing at the pain in his back. He shouted something about piss.

Instead of putting the ambulance back on the highway, he cocked his weapon and aimed at her.

"You were supposed to be in the hospital with a bullet wound to the leg," he said.

She kicked her feet and tried to right herself, but she didn't have the strength. Her feet moved as if underwater.

"Here's your bullet wound."

The gun roared. She felt the impact but not much else. Blood formed in a circle on her jeans where a small black hole opened mid-thigh. She panicked, her mind screaming, eyes wide, but she still couldn't move.

"You fucking bitch," Frank shouted. "How the hell did you think you could beat me?"

She chuckled at the insanity of the moment and the position she found herself in. The pain had not reached her consciousness yet.

"Thanks," she said. "I needed that."

She gave her best effort to right herself again, but nothing worked. "Dammit. You think you could help me up here? I still need to kill you."

"I will give you this." He winced again as he looked in the rearview mirror. "You are one of the strangest, toughest opponents I have ever met."

"This leg wound will heal. I've been shot before." She met his gaze. "But you can't heal fucked. That's you."

"Goodbye, Sarah. Say hey to the big guy when you get there."

He lined up the gun with her eyes. She could see down the small hole of the barrel.

The weapon firing in the cab of the ambulance was deafening.

Chapter 58

THREE DAYS LATER ...

Parkman sipped a much-needed coffee at Umbertide's police headquarters. He had barely slept since 'the night of the arrests' as the media had dubbed it.

Antonio Delarusso of the state police was arrested in his home without incident. The Minister of Finance, Silvio Capelli, was arrested in his hotel room in Umbertide, along with two of his aides. Charges stemmed from their involvement with Sam "The Dealer" Marconi, a known hitman and Cosa Nostra associate, in addition to other charges relating to the transfer of funds from a large GMO corporation that had been promised they would be allowed to operate in Italy. They had already been growing GMO crops that were now slated for incineration.

But none of that was important to Parkman. What was

important to him was finding Sarah and the man everyone referred to as Frank De Luca, an alias. He had since learned De Luca's real name was Günter Sørensen, a Norwegian-born international assassin wanted by police agencies around the world.

"Tell me again," Parkman said. "What did the ambulance driver say happened?"

"He was ordered at gunpoint to drive," Kierian replied. "When he got on the highway, he jammed on the brakes and jumped out of the ambulance. Then he ran, screaming for help. Officers arrived two to three minutes later and secured the scene."

"This driver is claiming he didn't see anything else?"

Kierian shook his head and looked down at the table. "Nothing. He got drilled by one of their best interrogators. They believe that whatever happened in the ambulance was out of his sight. He has no idea what happened when he was running along the highway, looking for help."

"Tonight's his first day back on the job?"

Kierian nodded.

Parkman took the last sip of his coffee and set the empty cup on the table.

"Damn it," he said.

"What?"

"It's just not like Sarah."

Parkman pulled a toothpick out of his breast pocket and slipped it between his lips, spinning it back and forth. He had found some at a grocery store in town after the police had released him from his holding cell.

"She's been gone for three days, Parkman. No trace. They found a lot of blood on the passenger seat of the ambulance and matched it to Sarah's."

"They also found a substantial quantity of blood from another source that has yet to be identified."

Kierian nodded. "I know. But we're talking about Sarah's disappearance. Since you know her better than anybody, and you feel this is unlike her, where would she go? Do you think she's in hiding until this case is fully investigated so she can be absolved of any charges?"

"Maybe she's waiting for Aaron to be released," Parkman said as he glared at Kierian.

"You know as well as I do that Aaron was released two days ago, and all charges erased from his record. As an apology, the Toronto Police Services offered him the contract of training their new officers in hand-to-hand combat for the next two years. That's a highly coveted contract."

"Remind me what Aaron's answer was."

"He turned it down."

"I'm surprised after the way they treated him that he didn't just show them what hand-to-hand combat was on the spot."

"You know, Parkman, your sarcasm is so thick I can smell it."

"Kierian, I'm angry. You misled Sarah, brought her here under false pretenses, faked your own death, had her boyfriend put in jail on murder charges, and then probably got her killed as she tangled with an international assassin, and you're bothered by my sarcasm. You're the trained professional. You should've been the one out there fighting Günter, not Sarah."

"You think I don't know that?"

They glared at each other.

"I have to live with this each and every day," Kierian added.

"At least you get to live. We can't say that about Sarah."

"Does Sarah know anyone in Umbertide? How about Italy? When you two came here a few years ago, did she make any friends? Someone who would harbor her?"

Parkman twiddled with the toothpick and shook his head. "No one. We weren't here long enough to make friends. We arrived by train, met with an assault team, and left with them. We stayed one night in Umbertide."

"Then I have nothing, and neither do the Italian authorities. Sarah didn't have a passport. She didn't cross international borders. That leaves us with two options. One, she's dead—"

Parkman flinched.

"—or she's alive," Kierian continued, "and hiding somewhere in the eurozone."

"But she wouldn't hide out." Parkman pushed his chair back and got up to pace. "Sarah doesn't hide. She's afraid of nothing and no one. She wouldn't hide to wait out this investigation. Worse has happened to her. She would want her side heard."

"Then offer the authorities a plausible reason for her blood in the ambulance and disappearance."

"I can't." He looked at Kierian with pleading eyes. "I can't because," his voice cracked, "I fear the worst." He sat down. "And I'm the one who gets to tell her parents all this shit."

"I can come with you."

Parkman's head shot up fast. "It's better you don't."

Kierian nodded. "So that's it?"

"That's it. Until she surfaces, we're done here."

"When does your flight leave?" Kierian asked.

Parkman checked his email on his cell phone.

"Eleven tomorrow morning."

"Where are you staying tonight?"

"Rome."

"Me too."

They sat in silence for a few moments.

"I understand they agreed to keep us up to date if anything new develops," Kierian said.

Parkman nodded.

"You look deeply upset," Kierian said.

Parkman met his gaze, his eyes watering. "I've let Sarah down."

"You were being held prisoner by Delarusso. What could you do?"

"The circumstances don't matter. I was here. I came to help. Sarah's gone, and we know nothing. Now I'm leaving. However you add it up, I failed her."

Kierian reached across the table to touch Parkman's hand, but Parkman pulled away.

"Don't …"

Kierian got up and walked to the door.

"Let me know if you need anything."

He opened the door and left.

Parkman put his forehead on the metal table and wept.

"I'm sorry, Sarah. I'm so sorry."

Chapter 59

AARON CLOSED THE DOJO at seven in the evening and headed for the restaurant. Three of his martial arts teachers had planned a birthday dinner for him at a steakhouse called The Keg.

Since Sarah disappeared in Italy, they had been so supportive, always trying to get him out, buy him a drink, come over, watch a movie, or go golfing. Anything to get him out of the apartment. But Aaron wanted to stay near the phone.

Parkman called with routine updates as he stayed in touch with that asshole Kierian. But there had been nothing new in two months. No sign of Sarah, alive or dead.

The bad news was there had been no sign of Günter Sørensen, aka Frank De Luca, either. The idea that Sarah was holding him somewhere wasn't popular. It was more probable that he did something to Sarah and disappeared.

But nothing had been found or proven to enable a single scenario that the authorities could sink their teeth into.

It was June, two full months since Sarah had left for Italy, and still no sign of her.

Aaron walked down Jarvis Street on his way to The Keg with Sarah on his mind. Sarah was always on his mind.

He had attended the funeral her parents had for Sarah in Santa Rosa without the body as the Italian authorities finally deduced that the amount of blood found in the ambulance was enough that Sarah was probably deceased. Not many people could survive after losing nearly four pints. The average adult had only eight to ten pints of blood.

In the last two months, Aaron had come to terms with Sarah's disappearance. Even if she were up to something, she would've called him. She would've told him. If she stayed away to protect the people she loved from some unseen enemy, she wouldn't contact her parents, but she would call him. She knew he could handle himself.

But no call came.

His step faltered when he saw the lights of The Keg and knew who was in there, waiting for him.

His friends. Wanting him to enjoy himself. Wanting him to break from the shell that he constructed around himself.

Did he deserve to have fun? What would Sarah think if she saw him laughing and drinking and eating just nine weeks after she fought an assassin to the death in an ambulance in Italy?

His knees buckled. Aaron fell to the sidewalk, his stomach clenching.

"Sarah …" he whispered her name.

It felt like the thousandth time he whispered it today,

down from weeks before. After teaching the green belts in their nightly classes, students would come up to him and ask who Sarah was. He had been saying her name over and over when he would kiai.

"Are you okay, Mister?" a man in a suit and tie asked as he walked past.

Aaron nodded and used a street sign's post to get to his feet.

Across the street, a woman walked south on Jarvis, her blonde hair blowing in the cool evening breeze.

"Sarah …" he whispered her way.

She turned to him and smiled.

"Sarah!" he shouted.

Aaron launched off the ground and ran into the street.

A horn blared, tires screeched. The bumper of a car smacked his thigh as it stopped. Aaron kept on his feet but faltered and turned to the car. The driver hopped out.

"Are you fucking crazy?" the driver shouted. "I could have killed you."

Aaron looked back at the blonde girl on the other side of the street, but she was gone, with only two high-school-aged teens and an older woman with a child in tow.

"What's wrong with you?" the driver asked.

He went to push Aaron off the road.

Aaron deflected the man's hand, spun left, and ducked under his extended arm. He ended up behind the man, who turned around to face him.

"You're crazy," the driver said and walked back to his open car door.

Aaron checked the road to make sure it was clear of traffic before crossing. He couldn't exist having visions of

Sarah. He couldn't exist locked in depression. Grief had overpowered him. First, he lost his sister, and now Sarah. Two women he loved deeply were taken from him in a few short years.

Any other man would crumble, but Aaron realized in that second that he needed to collect himself up and be strong. What if Sarah was okay? What if she came back one day? What would she say if she saw him now?

It was time to get back to living because anything else was dying, and he wasn't ready to die yet.

He strode to the restaurant's door and entered the well-lit lobby of The Keg.

He was told his friends were waiting for him on the second floor.

He walked up the stairs and searched for their table but didn't see them right away.

Someone touched his elbow. A cold piece of metal rested against the base of his neck.

"The mess will make these fine folks vomit if you move, and I have to pull this trigger."

Sarah!

He went to turn around, but the hand gripping his elbow tightened, and the metal piece pushed harder into the nape of his neck.

"You don't listen well."

His heart raced, his pulse gyrating. "It's never been one of my stronger suits."

The metal pulled away, and the hand on his elbow let go.

"Turn around and hug me like you've never hugged me before. Oh, how I've missed you, fucker."

Aaron spun and stared into the eyes that had haunted him

for months. He took a sharp breath, opened his arms, and passed out.

***

"You made us miss a lovely meal at The Keg. I wanted to order a juicy prime rib."

Sarah?

He opened his eyes.

Sarah looked down at him. The real, the only, the alive, Sarah Roberts.

"What?" he asked. "How?"

She touched his lips with her finger. "Shhh. All in good time."

"I deserve to know." He sat up. They were in his living room.

"Daniel and Benjamin helped carry you up."

"What happened? At least some of the basics. You were gone for months. We thought you were dead."

"It's better if the world still thinks so."

"Why?"

"Long story." Sarah limped to the balcony doors.

"What's wrong with your leg?"

"Bullet to the thigh. Almost healed."

"Sarah." He sat up. "Please. Give me the abbreviated version, then."

She faced him. It was dark outside. He couldn't see her face, only her silhouette.

"You've heard of The Cowboy?"

Aaron nodded. "His work has gone international and gotten a lot of people arrested."

"He sent out an email."

"I heard about it."

"This email was intercepted and read by a friend and his wife. Consider this friend a man who believes in survival of the fittest."

"He's a believer in Darwinism?"

"Exactly. Well, this friend read the email, showed up at the hospital, and stayed on the sidelines as the police cordoned off the area. When I left in an ambulance, he gave chase. He pulled in front of the ambulance and made the driver slam on his brakes. The bad guy—"

"De Luca? Parkman told me."

"Yeah, him. De Luca bested me and was about to shoot me when our friend shot him. I was already wounded in the leg."

"They said you lost almost four pints of blood."

"It felt like more." Sarah walked to the armchair and sat down. "This friend took me in his car and threw De Luca's body in his trunk. We left before the police showed up."

"Where have you been for two months?"

"Recuperating at this friend's home. De Luca was buried out there. No one will ever find De Luca's body, and you can never repeat any of this."

"Why haven't you told the authorities?"

"I can't reveal the identity of my friends."

"Why?"

"They have enemies throughout the world. Think of them as someone like me who often gets mixed up in things bigger than them. They got away and are secure now. If anything happens to threaten them, he will take on De Luca's image and deal with it. Through my friend, The Ghost will live on."

"But how? What happened to you?"

"They nursed me back to health. I was shot, spent, and used up. I slept for almost two weeks straight. Then the physiotherapy was another form of hell, but here I am. I'm back. Only you and my parents will know for now. I need quiet, calm, and time off."

"I can understand that. You've been going for a long time. Have you told Parkman?"

She nodded. "I called him when I returned."

"How did he take it?"

"Somewhat like you. But then he told me to watch my back."

"Why? What now?"

"He wouldn't tell me over the phone. Said he would come to Toronto next week to tell me what's going on."

"That doesn't sound good."

"Doesn't matter. Kierian and his band of fuckups—"

"You mean the authorities?"

"Yeah, fuckups, like I said. They all think I'm dead. I want to leave it like that as long as I can. There's something to what Frank De Luca taught me."

"What's that?"

"Being a ghost has its advantages."

Aaron leaned back on the couch and wiped his face with his hand. "What did you place against the back of my neck in the restaurant?"

"This." Sarah held up a lipstick container. "Hilarious, right?"

"No. Not so much."

"I've missed you, Aaron."

"You have a funny way of showing it. No call for two

months."

"We have a lot of making up to do." She got up from the armchair. "Come with me. Let me show you how much I've missed you."

He followed her toward the hallway.

"I'm curious about this friend of yours."

"Curiosity will get you killed." She stopped halfway down the hall. "Do you want to die?" she asked in her bedroom voice.

"Stupid question."

"Then don't be curious. Stupid question for someone who knows better. Aaron, be quiet and do what you're told. Don't be stupid, and I won't hurt you."

"Oh, Sarah, you're truly back, aren't you?"

"Shut up and take me to bed. Or would you rather watch TV, go for a walk or stare into space and think about insects."

"Random."

She raised her eyebrows, waiting for an answer.

"Let's go." He passed her and entered the bedroom. In the darkened room, he didn't see her dive at him. They landed in a heap on the bed, Sarah giggling.

"It's good to have you back, woman."

"It's good to be back. But don't forget; it's safer if I remain dead."

"Got it. You're dead."

She kissed his mouth. "No, you're dead."

Then she rolled over and jumped on him.

Aaron realized at that moment that they were both very much alive and that he would never let anything happen to her ever again.

He would rather be dead.

Afterword

DEAR READER,

*Spoiler Alert—read only after you have read *The Rogue*.

Italy is a beautiful country to visit. During the research of this novel, I spent seven months in Italy, six of those in Umbertide. I ate at the Ristorante Capponi (renamed Ristorante Capitone in the novel) in the piazza called April 25. The food was amazing, and I recommend this intimate restaurant if you ever make it to Umbertide. I blew this restaurant up in *The Rogue* because it is, in fact, the only restaurant with a hotel above it in *centro storico*, the historical center of Umbertide, and I needed a hotel for Frank's bombs to be effective.

I've toured the entire area on the regional trains. I walked by the broken-down tobacco farm with the caved-in roof where Sarah found the bodies of the dead farmer and his wife. The house used in the farmer's field where the GMO conference was held was the house I lived in for four months in 2011 while researching *The Crypt*, another Sarah book that took place partially in Italy. The large bathroom actually had a window right beside the toilet that looked out from the second floor onto the huge fields in the back.

Many of the sites you visited in The Rogue were actual buildings and locations. The rest was fiction. For example, in Roma Termini, the train station in Rome, there is no train heading to Perugia—that's fiction. Yes, you can *take* a train to Perugia, but the Ancona train stops in Perugia on the way to Ancona. The sign Sarah read in Termini would not have said Perugia.

Sarah meeting Jonas Saul (me) was added for fun. When Darwin hears my name, he pauses, wondering why he knows it, too. I did this because I loved it and had a great time writing it. My hope is that it translates to the reader in a goodhearted way. I've read another author who wrote this in his novels, and every single time he did, I absolutely loved it. There was a time when Stephen King's movies included a cameo of him somewhere in the film. I remember going to the theater after reading the book first, of course, and waiting, watching for the chance to see him pop up for his bit part. Even Quentin Tarantino does it with his films.

Antico Giardino Caffè is a real coffee bar. Gabriele owns it and serves the best espressos in Umbertide. Because of his generosity and kindness, I featured his coffee bar in *The Rogue* out of respect. He actually has black curly hair, as the story says (although he's bald now, in 2022). I recommend stopping in if you ever get to Umbertide—say Jonas Saul sent you. Thanks, Gabriele, for many wonderful memories—you and your woman, Giamiaca, will not be forgotten.

Infomatica is the internet store in Umbertide. It exists, but not so much in *The Rogue* after the shootout there. I decided to destroy this store for fictional reasons, but man, sometimes the internet in Italy was atrocious! Sorry, but it's the truth. One of the biggest complaints I have about Italy is the internet. Don't come to Italy and expect high-quality access to the web unless you stay in Rome.

I had a blast writing this novel and received a massive amount of help from numerous people.

First, my amazing editor for this novel is Robb Grindstaff, a man I simply cannot live without. He's down to earth and not afraid to tell me what I need to work on, what works, and what needs to be deleted. I could not publish without him.

Second, my *insegnante d' Italiano*, or Italian language teacher, Francesco Candelori, was instrumental in ensuring the local dialect, vernacular, and Italian was perfect. Google Translate has nothing on this guy. He came to my Italian apartment weekly while I was in Umbertide to give me Italian lessons. If you're ever in Umbertide and want to learn the language, his number is posted all over town.

Now, I want to talk about GMOs. They are a real problem. Although the murder of the Italian Agricultural Minister was fictional, GMOs are killing people.

All data covered in *The Rogue* is real. They have injected the DNA of an Arctic flounder into the DNA of tomatoes. They have taken spider DNA and forced it into a goat's DNA to extract the web proteins from the goat's milk in order to produce better bulletproof vests.

Crops are laced with pesticides—nerve gas—that kills pests. What does it do to humans over time?

One Danish farmer said, "We won't be remembered as the generation who introduced science to the farmer's field, but as the generation who sacrificed our own children for the profits of a few multinational corporations."

Read about the whistle-blowing regulator in Brazil who claims all GMO approvals in his country are illegal:

http://www.naturalnews.com/041784_GMOs_regulators_Brazil.html

Join the conversation at Natural News and subscribe to the daily email—mind-blowing information:

http://www.naturalnews.com

Watch the trailer for "Food Matters" on YouTube, a movie I highly recommend:

http://www.youtube.com/watch?v=eFIwbDYxoEk

Watch the truth about GMOs explained in a ten-minute animated cartoon:

http://www.youtube.com/watch?v=KGqQV6ObFCQ

"The World According to Monsanto" is brutal:

http://www.youtube.com/watch?v=N6_DbVdVo-k

Then do more research on your own to examine how far and how bad this catastrophe has become.

This Afterword wouldn't be complete without a dedication to you. None of this is possible without you, the reader. So I leave you with the parting thought of how much I love and appreciate you.

Because of you, I'm eternally grateful.

Therefore, *The Rogue* is dedicated to you—yes, you—the person still reading this. May happiness find you wherever you are, and when life gets in the way and pisses you off, do what Sarah would do, minus the weapons, and go headfirst at the problem, solve it, and move on with life. Take care of yourself and the people you love. Stay strong and be well.

Until the next novel.

Yours,

Jonas Saul

About Jonas Saul

Jonas Saul is the bestselling author of the Sarah Roberts Series—more than two million sold!—and has written and published over sixty thrillers. After acquiring an agent, he signed several deals in Los Angeles, with MadRiver Pictures optioning his Sarah Roberts Series— over forty books!—(currently in development).

Jonas has often outranked Stephen King and Dean

Koontz on Amazon over the past decade. He's regularly invited to be a guest speaker, teacher, or workshop presenter at international writing conferences and film festivals worldwide. He hosts an annual writer's retreat in Greece, where he currently lives. He focuses his teaching on how to get tension and emotion in every scene, on every page, how he made it as a creator/writer, the path to success in this business, and the pitfalls to avoid. He also hosts a reading retreat in Greece with guest authors, yoga retreats, and hiking retreats. Visit the Imagine Greece Retreats website at www.imaginegreeceretreats.com, or email him directly to discuss an opportunity to join one of the retreats at jonas@imaginegreeceretreats.com.

Jonas is also a professional freelance editor. He works for several publishers and does private editing for clients, with many testimonials on his website at www.imaginepress.org, which details each author's response to Jonas's editing skills. Email Jonas directly for an editing quote at editor@imaginepress.org.

To book Jonas for a speaking engagement at a writer's conference/festival, to have him on your jury at a film festival, or even to say hello, email Jonas directly at jonassaul@icloud.com.

For updates on releases, hit the "Follow" button on Amazon or Bookbub, and join Jonas on Facebook, where he's most active.

Contact Jonas Saul

Linktree: Find me here

Email: jonassaul@icloud.com